Guilty Until Proved Innocent

J Walter Hodgson

Published by Hodgson Consulting

Dedication

To my wife Anyta

Our children and their partners

Caroline and Fraser, Chris and Sarah,

Katherine and Simon

and our grandchildren

Frankie, Alex, Gaby, Ben, Sam, Iestyn, Rhys and Finlay

Acknowledgement

Thank you to Barbara Tayabali for allowing me to use the name of her late husband, and my much missed friend Arif Tayabali, to represent one of the key characters.

To John Richard Schuster for his invaluable contribution, advice and editing skills.

Guilty Until Proved Innocent

Preface

Guilty Until Proved Innocent is a story of adultery and revenge.

The adultery is imagined. The revenge is real.

The story begins in Goa prison on the day that prisoner 5940 was due to be released after serving three years for a crime he never committed.

The prison superintendent handed the prisoner a large white envelope. The prisoner stared at it. It was addressed to Prisoner 5940 c/o Goa Prison. Goa, India. It was clear from the stamps in the top right corner, that it had been posted in the United States.

He turned the envelope over and looked at the return address. It was from Richard Dadson, a lawyer he'd never met, from Green Bay, Wisconsin, a place he'd never visited.

From his time inside he'd learned that the envelope would have been opened and re-sealed before he was allowed to read it. That was one of the many rules that shaped his life inside.

Holding the envelope in his left hand he used his right thumb to peel back the self-adhesive flap.

He paused. Took a deep breath and let out a long sigh. His hesitation was understandable. He had expectations, hope even, that this was going contain good news, but years behind bars had taught him to be cautious.

As he pulled the contents out of the envelope, the first thing that caught his eye was the Air New Zealand business class ticket from London to Los Angeles, flight number NZ001, seat number 5B. Date of departure 24th May 2015.

All being well, in two days' time he would be flying at 35,000 feet above the Atlantic Ocean on his way to a new life in America.

He checked the rest of the contents.

Two more airline tickets that would take him from Goa to Mumbai and from Mumbai to London.

There was $2,000 in cash and a Visa credit card with the name Michael J Hanson embossed on the front.

Last but not least, a temporary British passport. The photograph inside was identical to the one in his recently expired passport.

Above the photograph, in capital letters were the comforting words: UNITED KINGDOM OF GREAT BRITAIN AND NORTHERN IRELAND.

As he continued to check the other items, a woman in her late forties, sat in front of a laptop in an office in Oxford, England. She checked the information on the screen, studied it for a few seconds and then pressed print, leaned back in her chair as the printer whirled into life.

She watched as the Hewlett Packard all-in-one machine began to print an airline ticket. It was for an Air New Zealand flight NZ001 from London, Heathrow to Los Angeles. Seat number 5A. Date of departure 24th May 2015.

The holders of tickets 5A and 5B sat on opposite sides of the world, 5000 miles apart.

He in India, she in England.

In just two days they were destined to sit next to each other as strangers on a plane, embarking on a journey that would change their lives.

CONTENTS

CONTENTS

CHAPTER 1   Prisoner 5940

Friday 22nd May 2015 – Goa prison, India.

For many people Friday 22nd May would be just another day, but not for prisoner 5940.

This was the day he'd remember for the rest of his life. He was about to be released from prison after serving three years of a 12-year sentence for a crime he never committed.

He had been accused of murder. The victim was his wife.

The prison Superintendent handed him a certified copy of the judgement of the court of appeal.

Just a few formalities and he would be free to go.

The Superintendent placed two bags on the table, picked up one, and emptied the contents onto the table between them.

'These are your belongings. You need to check them and sign, to say that nothing is missing'.

The soon-to-be-released prisoner picked up his old leather wallet.

Inside were credit and store cards. Each one past its expiry date.

Sixty-four Rupees. At the current exchange rate of 66 Rupees to the US dollar, not enough for a cup of coffee.

Eighty-five US dollars. He hadn't seen the faces of George Washington or Abraham Lincoln for a very long time.

A three-year-old mobile phone. Old technology and worthless in today's high tech market.

His Rolex Oyster Perpetual watch. When he first arrived in prison he was told that it would be too dangerous to wear. The Rolex would be stolen within a week, and in the process, he could lose a hand.

He picked it up and stared at the face. The auto-wind mechanism of the precision made timepiece stirred into action. The watch awoke from a long sleep.

The second hand began to sweep slowly.

A Rolex watch is expensive. Maybe this was why.

The guard interrupted; 'Probably worth a lot more today than when you came in'.

The second package had been opened and re-sealed.

Inside was $2000 in cash and three business class flight tickets that would soon take him home to Los Angeles via Mumbai and London.

Next to the tickets was a temporary British passport and a credit card.

He was a British citizen who, until that fateful trip in April 2012, had lived for 10 years with his American born wife in Los Angeles.

For the last three years, Michael J Hanson had been known simply as prisoner 5940.

The home he hadn't seen for three years was a four bedroomed detached house in a leafy suburb on the outskirts of Los Angeles. It had been empty since the day he locked up to go on holiday with his wife, three years before.

A compliments slip from Richard Dadson, his American lawyer, had a one-line message on it.

Your card is good for $5000. Your four-digit PIN number is already known to you.

After his lawyer had written hundreds of letters and travelled from America to England to visit the British Foreign Office in London, came the reward for his dogged perseverance.

Prompted by the British Foreign Office, under pressure from Amnesty International and the European Court of Human Rights in Strasbourg, the Supreme Court of Justice in India, agreed for the case to be re-opened.

It had taken his lawyer twelve months of negotiating before he received news that his client was to be granted a full pardon.

The Supreme Court of India had overturned the original judgement and agreed his immediate release.

An international incident had been avoided.

In addition, the court agreed to Dadson's demand for compensation.

Prisoner 5940, would soon be on his way home to Los Angeles to collect a banker's draft for a little over $6 million dollars. Two million dollars for each year he'd spent behind bars, plus interest.

'Don't forget to take your wages' sneered the Superintendent, as he produced a wad of notes and counted them out. 'Seven hundred and fifty-four Rupees. If you'd prefer dollars we can do that for you'.

The prisoner looked up.

'I'd prefer dollars. I'm not planning to stay in India for any longer than is necessary'. He paused. Looked at the notes and said; 'Not much to show for three years work'.

It would have been more had he not squandered his wages on 16 tooth brushes, a zillion tubes of toothpaste and various other toiletries and treats from the prison shop.

'Oh, I almost forgot' said the Superintendent. 'Prisoner 5921 put in a request for me to give you this painting. He wants you to have as a parting gift'.

He held up an oil painting. The look on the superintendent's face spoke volumes.

He never wanted to see it again. He would have been happier to have seen it destroyed.

Prisoner 5940 stared at it and was moved by the gesture. He knew immediately who the final recipient would be.

'We'll wrap it for you so that it doesn't get damaged in the hold'.

CHAPTER 2   First step to freedom

Friday 22nd May 2015 – Goa prison, India.

As much as he never wanted to hear, see or use the numbers 5940 again, he recalled what Dadson had written on the compliment slip.

'Your four-digit PIN number is already known to you.'

He made a mental note to change it at the first opportunity.

As he stepped outside the heavy wooden prison gates he saw what the Superintendent had described as a courtesy car.

It looked a like a 1950's relic.

In appearance it reminded him of a British Morris Oxford. It was in fact a Hindustan Ambassador. One of the last to roll off the West Bengal production line in May 2014.

Shortly after the Tata Motor Group acquired the British tools in 1957 they began to produce their own version of the legendary car.

The top half of this particular one was painted a garish yellow like a New York taxi. Bottom half was dark green.

Even without the illuminated sign on the roof anyone could see that the prison courtesy car was, in fact, a local taxi.

The passenger door opened and out stepped the driver.

A second later 5940 remembered that in India, they drive on the left.

He stood there for a moment and hesitated. He looked up at the clear blue sky and inhaled. The air smelt different.

Life in prison had been predictable and to a degree, safe. Now, alone in a foreign country he felt vulnerable, apprehensive and slightly scared.

As he took his first step to freedom, he recalled the immortal words of Astronaut Neil Armstrong when he stepped down from Apollo 11 to become the first man to stand on the surface of the moon. On 20th July 1969 125 million viewers heard him say:

'One small step for man. One giant leap for mankind'.

As prisoner 5940 took his first step to freedom on Friday 22nd May 2015, he had an audience of one. An unknown taxi driver in a town virtually unheard of in America. Even those who had heard of Goa would be hard pushed to place it on a map.

The state of Goa has a population of 1.6 million, most of whom live in the state capital Panjim which lies on the coast. It has been described as the 'pearl of the Orient'.

As the car drove off it joined the long line of slow moving traffic that defines India. The passenger observed that the choice of colours for cars in India was limited to three, maybe four, but certainly not five.

The driver turned and asked; 'Goa airport, right?'

'Right'.

Amongst the locals, Goa International airport is more commonly known as Dabolim Airport, but most tourists refer to it as Goa. Nobody objects.

The journey could take anything from 30 to 90 minutes. Traffic chaos was an accepted way of life in India. Slow moving ox carts trundled through a mass of honking cars, taxis, buses, scooters and Tuk Tuks.

The driver didn't attempt to make conversation. He had made the journey before and knew that his passenger would probably not want to engage in idle chit-chat. He would have more important things on his mind. He'd appreciate some quiet time to contemplate what lay ahead.

As they drew level with a street market, something caught the passenger's eye.

'Driver, can you stop here for a minute? I won't be long'.

He leapt out and stepped briskly to the stall selling an assortment of brooms, brushes, plastic buckets and kitchen pots and pans. The stall holder looked up with a welcoming smile.

'I'd like to buy a mop, but I don't need the handle'.

The stall holder picked up a screwdriver. Unscrewed the metal band that secured the mop head to the handle. As he handed the mop head to his first customer of the day, his customer looked on as the handle was propped up against a sign on the stall which read Genuine Fake Watches. Lifetime Guarantee.

He accepted the full price of 60 Rupees. He was happy. He'd just sold a mop head at full price and now had a spare handle, which he would sell later that day.

On arriving at the airport the driver once again emerged from the passenger side. His passenger wondered what it would feel like to drive a car again.

There was no charge for the government courtesy car.

At the airport, 5940 made his way through customs and passport control to board an Air India internal flight from Goa to Mumbai.

Exactly one hour and fifteen minutes later he would see the lights of Mumbai Airport, known officially by its Indian name: Chhatrapati Shivaji International Airport.

He smiled to himself. A word with two aitches could come in handy in a game of Scrabble, in most parts of the world, but probably not in Delhi or Mumbai.

He would spend his first night of freedom at the Hyatt Regency Hotel booked and paid for by the Indian Government. A final gesture from his host of three years, anxious to see him leave.

The next morning, he was booked on an Air India non-stop flight to London.

He checked his itinerary which Dadson had placed in the envelope with the tickets.

Saturday 23rd May 2015 Air India flight 131 was due to depart from Mumbai at 13:05 and arrive in London the same day at 18:10.

He would stay overnight at the Hilton hotel.

For the second time in two days he would sleep in a luxury king-size bed.

On Sunday 24th May he would take the hotel courtesy bus to London Heathrow airport's Terminal 2.

CHAPTER 3   Passenger 5A

Sunday 24th May 2015

London Airport Heathrow. Terminal 2. Departure lounge.

The lady holding Boarding Pass 5A for Air New Zealand Flight NZ001 from London to Los Angeles was smartly, but casually dressed.

She was not looking forward to the prospect of spending 12 hours in a seat, however comfortable, next to a complete stranger.

5A was in her late forties. Intelligent, articulate and attractive to both sexes.

She could have been a fashion designer or fashion consultant. In her designer jacket and trousers she could have graced the cover of Vogue.

Her immaculately coiffured hair suggested regular visits to an expensive hairdresser.

She could wear an on old pair of jeans and a loose fitting sweater and men would still find her attractive.

Married women often found her threatening. Men found her slightly intimidating.

For most men, 5A had everything a woman, or a man could wish for. Looks, style, a figure to die for, and a dazzling smile.

From her appearance one might assume that she could have any man she wanted, but she was single, never been married, and had no desire to. She was happy and content with her life.

5A had lived the life of a woman in a man's world.

She'd studied Chemical Engineering at Homerton College, Cambridge and graduated with a BA honours degree.

After graduating, she joined the Royal Air Force and rose rapidly through the ranks to become Pilot Officer, then on to Squadron Leader flying fast jets.

A woman in a man's world. The nickname given to her by her fellow pilots was Dickless. She rather liked it. Pilot Officer Treblecock was known as Thriceblest.

She flew her RAF Tornado in combat missions in Afghanistan and Iraq.

At the time she was the only female pilot in 9 Squadron. Without exception, all of her colleagues were young, fit, testosterone-charged individuals who thrived on excitement and challenge.

After serving for eight years in the Royal Air Force, she resigned her commission and continued her love of flying in the relative safety of a Boeing 747 Jumbo passenger jet.

Two years as first officer and then a fully-fledged captain. Once again, a woman succeeding in a man's world.

Flying fast jets was thrilling. By comparison, flying a jumbo jet was less so but had its compensations.

There were always two qualified pilots in the cockpit, plus a flight engineer, giving the captain time to think and plan ahead.

Flying fast and low in theatre was always a white knuckle ride.

In a passenger jet tension peaks during take-off and landing. Statistically, most accidents occur during the three minutes after take-off and the three minutes prior to landing.

This is the time when flight crew need to be at their sharpest. Not so much tension, as heightened awareness.

The hours between wheels up and wheels down were mostly uneventful. Time when crew members would take it in turns to catch up on lost sleep.

As soon as the aircraft reached its cruising altitude of 35,000 feet the pilot would hand control over to George, aka the auto pilot. George took care of everything. Good old reliable George.

It wasn't long before long-haul flights became just a job, albeit a well-paid job.

In both careers she came to accept that being a woman in a predominantly male world, came at a price.

Sexist and risqué remarks, which would never be tolerated in civilian life, were par for the course among the flying fraternity. She took them all in good part. They were treated like water off a duck's back.

A large number of commercial pilots had gained their wings in the Royal Air Force. A small number had also flown fast jets in combat.

Following promotion to Captain the four gold braid bands on her cuffs confirmed to all that she was qualified to sit in the left hand seat.

After the doors of the aircraft closed she would welcome passengers aboard with a cheery; 'Good morning, ladies and gentlemen, boys and girls. This is your captain speaking'. She allowed herself a two second pause. Just enough time for the passengers to recognise the sound of a female voice. She would continue;

'As we prepare for take-off let me introduce you to your cabin staff today. They are here to make your flying experience an enjoyable one.

The weather today is expected to be fine and we estimate that we will arrive in Los Angeles on schedule. If you wish to adjust your watch the time in Los Angeles is 7:00 am local time. I'll speak to you again later. Meanwhile, sit back, relax and please watch the safety video'.

After three years of flying passenger jets, passenger 5A felt the need for more excitement and a new challenge. She gave up flying and joined CNN as a junior member of their outside broadcast unit.

True to form, she started at the bottom and quickly rose through the ranks.

Her innate ability to remain calm under stress, earned her respect from her colleagues and her bosses.

She came alive in front of a television camera, where she had to think on her feet, often working without a script.

She was the one who remained calm when the unexpected happened. Her crew trusted her judgement and had confidence in her.

On the day when 5A and 5B would meet for the first time, she was returning from a trip to England where she'd been reporting on the celebrations to mark the 70th anniversary of the VE (Victory in Europe) day.

The year coincided with the Queen Elizabeth becoming the longest serving British Monarch. More than sixty years on the throne, longer even than Queen Victoria.

The assignment went to 5A because she was from London and CNN believed her British accent would add something special to the report.

In her report she answered critics of the countywide street parties being held by quoting British Prime Minister David Cameron who said that the British were not celebrating the end of the war, but commemorating the lives of the millions of people, on both sides of the conflict. Millions had sacrificed their lives, so that the world would be a better and safer place.

The final edited version of 5A's report had been filed and sent to her office for transmission. By the time flight NZ001 touched down in Los Angeles, the story would already have been aired, and seen by millions of viewers across America and around the world.

After completing her assignment, 5A had stayed on in England to visit family and friends.

Her parents, Patricia and Al owned a successful pub called The Fox and Hounds.

The building dated back to the 16th century and as a Grade 2 listed building was protected by law from having internal or external structural alterations without planning permission. This was to ensure that original features would always be retained.

Among the many attractive features were oak beams and an inglenook fire place and when the logs were blazing away on a cold winter's day it was an effort to get up and venture outside.

The pub was in the picturesque village of Holmfirth on the edge of the Yorkshire moors.

The Fox and Hounds was a Free House which meant it was privately owned and not tied to a brewery. As a Free House the owner had complete freedom to buy supplies from whomever he chooses.

The highly respected and well supported typically English country pub had a reputation for offering a selection of real ales and down-to-earth food at reasonable prices.

A sign by the front door had the words Welcome to the Fox and Hounds - voted Best Pub Grub 2012, 2013 and 2014.

Real Ales aficionados had held their monthly meetings there for as many years as anybody could remember.

For 5A, one of her fondest childhood memories was the sight of horses and hounds gathered together for the traditional Boxing Day hunt held each year on 26th December. Americans didn't recognise Boxing Day but then the Brits never got around to celebrating Thanksgiving.

In the UK, the day after Christmas day is a public holiday when all sorts of sporting events take place. Most popular were football and horse racing, but unique to the English countryside, was the spectacle of the fox hunt.

Riders in their red, scarlet or black coats would sit proudly astride their horse and assemble for the 'meet' with a pack of baying and excitable hounds waiting for the cry Tally Ho when they'd be off chasing a scent.

As a child, 5A was intrigued by the quaint terms, rules and regulations that symbolised the elitist sport of fox hunting. Red and scarlet jackets were referred to as pinks and reserved for the master and senior members of the hunt.

Pinks originated from a fable of a tailor whose name was Mr Pinque. It's thought that the name caught on by accident but later used to demonstrate to outsiders that members of the hunt were in the know.

In the spring and summer, the moors were transformed into carpets of yellow and purple as the heathers came into full bloom. Not surprisingly, the area would be alive with groups of ramblers who used the pub as a stop off point.

Whenever she was at home, 5A would meet up with her old school friends, Mary, Tom and Amy, who still lived in the village.

Mary worked alongside her husband Harry, running the family-owned dairy. Their obsession with, and love of history was never in more evidence than when they insisted on delivering milk to the pub in old fashioned milk churns.

Tom was in IT. Nobody quite understood what that meant, but never liked to ask.

Tom's work regularly took him overseas. He claimed he was a husband-in-waiting. Waiting for the right girl to come along. Until then, he would enjoy life as a confirmed bachelor.

Amy was known to her friends as Amiable Amy. Everyone loved Amy. She was fun to be with, and lead singer of a folk band which she claimed was on the verge of a big break. Amy was the eternal optimist and everyone who knew her wanted her to succeed. Amy's enthusiasm was infectious.

5A liked to go home whenever she could because she was reminded of her roots which comprised simple values, kind people and life at a leisurely pace.

An altogether far cry from living in the fast lane in Los Angeles, California, but for all the pleasure she got from going home, she knew in her heart of hearts, that she could never go back permanently.

She had learned to live with the remarks from British friends who detected a slight American accent. Back at CNN, her American colleagues envied her British accent.

Home was a two-bedroom apartment on the outskirts of Los Angeles. Her American friends referred to it as a condo or condominium. She preferred apartment.

The apartment had nice views which improve at night, and was situated on the 3rd floor overlooking the city.

The décor was modern, furnishings understated and elegant. Visitors had been heard to describe it as stylish, and tastefully furnished, with a feminine touch.

CHAPTER 4   Passenger 5B

Sunday 24th May 2015

London Airport Heathrow. Terminal 2. Departure lounge.

As the hotel courtesy bus dropped him off, the passenger with minimum luggage made his way to the check-in desk.

Passenger 5B had a full head of dark hair with a hint of grey at the temples, giving him a rather distinguished appearance. He looked to be in his mid to late forties.

He weighed around 160 pounds, wore light blue chinos, a crisp white shirt and a tan-coloured casual jacket.

5B was travelling light. No inflight bag or laptop. He owned neither.

The only bag he held was plastic with the name W H Smith printed on both sides. The oil painting had been checked in at Mumbai and would be waiting for him in Los Angeles.

Inside the plastic bag were two books. 'A Long Walk to Freedom' by Nelson Mandela and 'A Prison Diary' by Jeffrey Archer.

His casual manner and appearance gave no hint to the fact that he had spent the last three years in an overcrowded prison in India, for a murder he hadn't committed.

5B was on his way home, without his wife.

He didn't even know if his wife was still alive.

On the 30th May 2012 a High Court Judge had sentenced him to 12 years in prison.

Three years into his 12 year sentence he was unexpectedly set free.

At the time of his release, the prison superintendent said that Britain's Prime Minister David Cameron, had intervened, but wouldn't elaborate.

CHAPTER 5   The nightmare begins

Thursday 26th April 2012

Goa beach hotel.

On that fateful day in April 2012, Michael Hanson had been enjoying a vacation with his wife Emily whom he'd married in Oxford, England 10 years earlier.

He took up a teaching post at California's UCLA (University of California, Los Angeles) as a lecturer in English literature.

The choice of Goa, when for the same money they could have gone to London, Paris or Rome for their first overseas holiday, would become central to the police enquiry.

His wife Emily knew that her choice of Goa would be a game changer. Michael thought it was a joint decision.

The point was later to be picked up by the prosecutor and used to convince a jury that in all probability the defendant was guilty of pre-meditated murder.   His wife had gone missing and presumed to be dead.

Knowledge gained by Emily as a junior partner in a law firm had proved to be invaluable.

She knew exactly how to track down a missing person. A skill which her husband would soon wish he shared.

Four days into their holiday they spent the morning by the pool.

He sat with a book. She with a Kindle.

This was their first holiday together outside America. The first time they'd had to carry a passport since flying from London to Los Angeles as newlyweds in September 2002.

At around 11.00 am on Thursday 26th April 2012 they were seen to be having an 'exchange of words'.

Emily Hanson was seen by witnesses to pick up her belongings and walk back to the hotel, alone.

Nothing in her actions or demeanour gave cause for concern, or a hint of what was to follow.

Later, eye-witnesses would state, under oath, and before a jury, that what they'd seen was a couple having a blazing row by the side of the hotel pool.

They described the scene as hostile, arms waving, accompanied by shouting.

It ended with the woman storming back to the hotel in a rage. They had witnessed a major incident.

The wife was seen entering the elevator and presumed to have returned to her room.

She was never seen again.

Her husband didn't report her missing until the next day.

CHAPTER 6   Police enquiry

Friday 27th April 2012

After he contacted the police to report his wife missing, a police constable, accompanied by a female officer from Goa Police station, visited the hotel.

They asked permission to search the room. Michael Hanson didn't object.

The room, described in the brochure as "large, spacious, overlooking manicured gardens with a magnificent panoramic view of the sea", matched the description.

They found the wife's mobile phone, purse and other personal belongings sitting on a bedside table.

According to her husband, nothing appeared to be missing.

A brightly coloured leather-effect passport holder was in full view. Inside the holder was her passport and the stub of the boarding card for the flight from Los Angeles.

The purse contained 53 dollars in notes, five credit and store cards.

There was no sign of a forced entry. There was no visible damage to the door or windows.

The hotel and its grounds were searched from top to bottom.

The hotel guest it seemed, had disappeared…vanished into thin air.

The officers questioned why she would go out alone and leave behind all her belongings. It didn't make sense.

Where had she gone and more importantly, where was she now?

She never tried to get in touch with her husband.

The amnesia theory was briefly considered, discounted and put on the back burner. They could come back to it later if necessary.

Had she left suddenly of her own free will?

Was she accompanied?

So many questions. None answered.

The CCTV tapes didn't help. They'd been accidentally wiped clean by a new member of staff, allegedly.

The husband appeared to be concerned but not unduly worried.

He was calm, as if he fully expected his wife to return at any minute. He even apologised for calling the police. He would make sure that when his wife did eventually return he would see to it that she made a full apology for wasting police time.

The police constable said that it wasn't unusual for foreigners to be abducted and held for ransom.

'There was nothing about that in the brochure', he thought.

He was advised to remain in his room and wait to be contacted.

No contact was made that day.

The next day Saturday 28th April, he showed the first signs of becoming agitated. He paced the floor of the large room. Whenever he heard a female voice, he would dash to the window.

Morning became afternoon. No contact.

Afternoon became evening. No contact.

He spent the next few hours staring at three phones, willing at least one of them to ring.

The hotel phone sat by the bedside. His and his wife's mobile phones were each plugged into a charger.

After three days he cancelled their flights home and extended their stay by a week, convinced that she would re-appear at any time.

The phones never rang. No sound or vibration to indicate a text message had arrived.

New guests checked in and moved into vacant rooms.

The hotel restaurant was full of new faces. New arrivals who knew nothing of the drama of the last few days.

Michael Hanson remained in his room for most of Sunday. Still no contact.

On the morning of Monday 30th April 2012 he became aware of the silent flashing of the hotel telephone. It was 6:00am.

The red light indicated that he had a message. He called reception.

They said he was to call a local number.

Whoever had left the message didn't leave a name.

He dialled the number.

Police Sergeant Patel was on duty.

Could he come down to the station?

No, they hadn't heard from the abductors.

They offered to send a car to pick him up.

He accepted.

CHAPTER 7   Interview room

Monday 30th April 2012

Sergeant Patel's superior was waiting in the interview room. He looked stern.

He leant forward and pressed a button on a recording machine. A red light came on.

The interview was being recorded, just like in the movies, although this was no movie. This was real.

He explained that in all his years as a police officer he had never known of a case of abduction where it had taken five days for a ransom demand to arrive.

He announced, with regret, that they had ceased enquiries into the abduction theory.

They would not pursue the matter further. The husband interrupted. But what about my wife?

Sergeant Patel continued; 'Nobody answering your wife's description has been seen leaving the hotel, taking a taxi, boarding a bus or checking in at the airport.

In any event, without a valid passport she couldn't have got through Passport Control. There was no evidence to suggest she might have taken her own life. No suicide note.

'To the best of our knowledge, you were the last person to speak to her.

According to the hotel guests sitting near you, you were arguing'.

'We exchanged a few words, yes, but I'd hardly call it arguing' retorted Hanson.

The officer stood up, faced the husband and said;

'So, Mr Hanson, you maintain that from the moment your wife went back to the hotel, you haven't seen or heard from her. She didn't call you and you haven't made any attempt to call her'.

'Why would I? She didn't have her phone with her. It's there on the table where she left it' he said, indignantly, pointing at the table.

The officer paused.

'We've contacted all hospitals within a 50-mile radius. They have no record of seeing or treating a female patient who matches your wife's description. Can you see why, as the only suspect, you are the prime suspect?

I am going to repeat to you what you have told us so far. Please listen carefully and stop me if I miss anything or misquote you'.

The red light remained on.

'You have told us that shortly after your wife returned to your room, you ordered a light lunch by the pool and didn't leave the area until approximately 15:30.

At that time, you went back to your room.

Your wife wasn't there and you assumed she had gone out for a walk or to the nearby shops. You had no reason to be alarmed.

At 18:00 hours you went down to the bar next to the dining room and sat alone.

You decided to have dinner sent up to your room and wait for your wife to return.

Is that correct so far?'.

'Yes', he replied.

'You went to bed just before midnight and it wasn't until the next day, when your wife hadn't returned, that you became concerned. That was around 7:00 or 7:15.

That was on Friday 27th April. Today is Monday 30th and in the intervening three days there have been no sightings of your wife and no contact'.

And then, out of the blue came the killer question.

'Why did you choose to have a holiday in India?' and before he had time to respond, the officer followed up with:

'This was the first time you or your wife had taken a holiday outside America. You could have gone to Europe. London, Paris or Rome but you chose Goa, India. Why?'

After a slight hesitation, he blurted out.

'It was my wife's idea'.

'You see, what I find strange, and, forgive me, hard to believe, is that you and your wife came to India with the apparent intention of staying inside one hotel for two weeks.

Can you not see why most people find that rather odd?

Most tourists coming to India for the first time have a travel itinerary. You and your wife could have spent six months here and not seen half of all that India has to offer.

You could have enjoyed tiger-watching in Ranthambhore and Kanha national parks.

Delhi is a city with wonderful architecture, or you could have visited the tea plantations of Darjeeling and Sikkim or visited the Taj Mahal.

Instead, you booked a room in the same hotel for 14 days. Can you see why I am curious?'

'It's easy. My wife and I both lead very busy lives and need time to relax and unwind', replied Hanson.

Even as he said it he thought to himself. This is crazy. How did I let her persuade me that Goa was *the* place to go to?

'What was your wife's maiden name?

'Pardon?'

Without waiting for a reply, he added with a smirk.

'It was da Gama wasn't it?'

'What's that got to do with it?' asked an incredulous Hanson.

'We have examined your wife's laptop. It seems that she has been researching her family history, for over a year. Before she married she shared her name with one of the world's most famous maritime explorers, Vasco da Gama?'

Hanson frowned quizzically, but said nothing.

The Sergeant continued: 'Vasco da Gama was the first person to sail from Portugal to India. 1497, I believe.

We have a port named after him. The da Gama name is revered in India'.

Hanson remained silent. Dumbstruck by the revelation that his wife could have spent more than a year, secretly researching her family ancestry, without mentioning it once.

The Sergeant continued with his summary.

'If your wife had taken her own life, her body would have been found by now.

The inevitable conclusion is that she or her body is still in the country'.

The mood in the room changed. The husband was startled to hear the word body, not once, but twice.

The Sergeant was joined by another police officer who sat down and said nothing.

A witness was required to be present for what was to follow.

The Sergeant began the well-rehearsed routine that preceded a formal charge and arrest.

He began;

'We found a travel brochure for India which we believe you brought with you. It was in your belongings. The page for the hotel you are staying in is turned down at the corner.

'I believe that for reasons best known to you, it was you, not your wife, who chose to come to Goa'. He paused.

'Before I go on is there anything you'd like to tell me?

Do you have anything to add that might explain what happened to your wife?'

Hanson was speechless. His mind was racing but not connecting with his mouth. No words came out.

'Michael Hanson, I am arresting you on suspicion of murder. You are not obliged to say anything but anything you do say may be taken down and used in evidence against you.

Do you understand?'

He was handcuffed and led to an adjacent room used as a temporary holding cell.

Although warm outside, the room felt cold, with a musty smell, as if it hadn't been used for some time.

There were no windows. Walls were painted white and the furniture consisted of three chairs and a small wooden table.

Hanson was asked to take a seat while the paperwork was completed.

He sat and watched as the two officers produced sheaves of papers and forms with tick boxes.

They diligently went through the pile of papers and signed the last one to confirm that they had followed the correct procedure.

The prisoner was invited to read them. He declined.

When asked, he declined the offer of a lawyer too.

He knew he hadn't done anything wrong. After all, he thought, only guilty people need a lawyer.

He fully expected his wife to turn up at any minute and for the charge to be dropped.

She never appeared.

He was remanded in custody for a month.

'Do you honestly believe I murdered my own wife?' he asked his captors.

'That's not for me to decide. That will be for a jury to decide'.

He was handcuffed and escorted through a door that led to a walled car park at the rear of the police station.

There, waiting for him, was an unmarked police van, ready to take him to Goa prison where he would be held in custody until a court appearance could be arranged.

He climbed in through the rear door and sat alone as the door was closed and bolted.

He'd seen it all on TV a million times before, with hopeful photographers running alongside, taking pictures through darkened windows.

For Michael Hanson there was nobody there to see him off.

No photographers and no cameras.

Nobody was interested in him.

CHAPTER 8   One month later - the trial

Wednesday 30th May 2012

Michael Hanson had been held in police custody for a month.

On the morning of the trial he was taken in an unmarked police van to the Crown Court where he was ushered in through a rear door, up a single flight of stairs to the court where a jury was already seated.

He was nervous, naturally, but remained confident that when a jury heard his side of the story and without any evidence against him, they would find him not guilty and free to go.

He hadn't reckoned on the prosecutor, Arif Tayabali, an impressive figure in his wig and black robes.

He was a formidable lawyer, who would leave no stone unturned in his search for truth and justice. He rarely lost a case.

The 12 jurors listened attentively, as Mr T, as he was known in the profession, outlined the seriousness of the case and the charges against the defendant.

He asked them to put to the back of their mind any thoughts thoy hold of an idyllic happily married couple enjoying a holiday together. He reminded them that a woman was missing presumed dead, and they would be expected to listen to the evidence and then decide whether or not a murder had been committed.

Each word was chosen carefully and delivered in an uncompromising manner.

He took his time, and emphasised each word or phrase to maximum effect. The power of his voice and delivery was unmistakably that of a well-educated man, utterly convinced that the defendant was guilty.

The jury sat spellbound. Richard Burton couldn't have been more compelling.

He made sure to look each juror in the eye as he spoke. They listened intently, hardly daring to move. It was an impressive performance, worthy of an Oscar, but this was no Hollywood movie and they knew it.

He quoted from police reports, hotel employees, eyewitness accounts, and when he finally got to the defendant's account of what happened, he systematically and methodically destroyed it as that of a fantasist with a hidden agenda.

With each word, Michael Hanson regretted not having his own lawyer, but it was too late.

Tayabali approached the jury.

'The defendant claims that it was his wife who chose Goa for their holiday', he declared.

'One might wonder why a woman of some taste, would forego the chance of going to London, Paris or Rome, and instead, chose to spend two full weeks in a single hotel in Goa.

'Does it not strike you as strange that the defendant, on his first visit to our beautiful country, would not visit at least one of the great tourist attractions we have to offer?

'I have here a brochure found in the defendant's hotel room. It has photographs of the Taj Mahal, tea plantations, night life in Mumbai. There can be no doubt that the defendant knew of the many other places they could have gone to. Indeed, it's possible that Mrs Hanson fully expected to visit some of them.

'You are being asked to believe that they travelled half-way around the world to sit by a pool,' he paused 'and unwind?'

The jurors sensed what was coming.

'There can be only one reason why the couple never ventured outside the hotel. The defendant had no intention of sightseeing but *every* intention of killing his wife and disposing of the body.

'Mr Hanson is guilty. Mrs Hanson remains missing presumed dead'.

As he neared the end of his submission he reminded the jury that they must listen to the Judge's summing up and, based on the evidence, decide who they believed was telling the truth.

His words were delivered with passion and emotion.

By including an oblique reference to the Judge, the inference was that the Judge shared his view. The Judge looked across and scowled.

'The defendant had every opportunity to murder his wife and dispose of the body. Of that there is no doubt.

One can only speculate over the seriousness of the issue of the exchange of words by the hotel pool. The defendant sticks to his claim that there was no argument but against that there are signed affidavits from five witnesses who described what they saw as 'a heated argument, bordering on violence'.

If you allow the defendant to walk free a terrible injustice will have been done.

The missing Mrs Hanson deserves more than that.

I submit to you that only by returning a verdict of guilty as charged will justice be seen to have been done.

With that Arif Tayabali sat down. He was the perfect example of an accomplished lawyer who had done his homework.

The saying 'fail to prepare or prepare to fail' had been clearly demonstrated. Tayabali was prepared. Michael Hanson was unprepared, and about to pay the price.

The Judge removed his reading glasses to address the jury;

'Members of the jury. You've heard the arguments both for and against.

In the absence of a body I must draw your attention to the points of law that are relevant to this case.

In the first instance one needs to have proof that an individual was alive. Of that, there is no doubt. Mrs

Hanson checked into the hotel and was seen by staff and guests.

Next, evidence is required to show that normal behaviour by the victim has stopped suddenly and completely.

We have that too. Since the moment she went missing, there is no evidence to suggest that Mrs Hanson carried out or attempted to carry out any of her usual activities. No phone calls. No emails or text messages. No use of the internet or laptop. No bank transactions and no record of contact made with friends or relatives.

If, after considering all the facts, you may decide that, even without any evidence of a body being found, the most likely cause for Mrs Hanson's sudden disappearance is that she was murdered.

If that is your decision you may return a verdict of guilty as charged.

The accused has not been able to prove his innocence.

He has relied almost entirely on lack of evidence.'

All eyes were focussed on the judge as he began his summing up.

'Members of the Jury' he said.

'Over the last two days you have listened to arguments from both sides. You have heard from eye-witnesses who claim that the 'exchange of words' as Mr Hanson put it was in fact a fully blown argument.

You must decide who you believe was telling the truth. The defendant or five eye-witnesses'.

He reminded them of their duties as members of the jury and not to discuss the case with anybody outside the jury room.

'You will shortly be escorted to a nearby room where you may take as much time as you require to weigh up all the evidence before coming to a unanimous decision.

I now need to draw your attention to two important facts.

You may have heard of occasions when courts allow a majority verdict.

That is not the case today. In the event that you are unable to reach a unanimous verdict you must convey that to the clerk of the court and await further instructions.

The second point is this. You will have been aware that throughout the trial the defendant chose not have a lawyer but to represent himself. That is his right.

It is not for you to decide if that was a wise decision or not. Your decision with regard to his guilt or otherwise of the charge of murder, must be based entirely on facts and facts alone'.

When you have adjourned to the jury room you must elect one person to act as foreman of the jury.

From then on, should you have any questions or seek clarification on a point of law, the foreman will convey that in writing and hand it to the court official.

With that, the twelve jurors were ushered out of the court and into an adjoining room.

The centre piece of the room was a long polished wooden table surrounded by chairs.

On the table were glasses, water jugs, writing pads and pens.

The jurors arranged themselves in two groups of six sitting opposite each other.

Four hours later they arrived at a unanimous verdict. The foreman informed the clerk and the court was quickly reconvened.

The clerk of the court asserted his authority.

'All rise in court' and with that the Judge reappeared from a side door and took his seat in the same winged chair he'd occupied for the last two days.

The foreman of the jury handed a piece of paper to the clerk who took it to the Judge.

The foreman remained standing while the rest of the jury sat in the same seats they'd occupied earlier.

The Judge looked directly at the foreman and asked if the jury had reached a unanimous verdict.

They had.

'Do you find the accused guilty or not guilty?'

For what seemed like an eternity, but was probably no more than a few seconds, Michael Hanson searched the faces of the jurors for a sign or clue of the decision.

Some jurors sat stony-faced, others stared at the judge while the eyes of the remainder flitted between the judge and the defendant.

If apprehension was a noise it would be deafening.

Michael Hanson braced himself as the verdict was read out.

'Guilty', said the foreman quickly followed by murmurings of approval from the public gallery.

The judge reminded everyone that even in the absence of a body, an individual could still be found guilty of murder.

As if to make doubly certain the Judge leant forward and asked:

'Was that a unanimous decision?'

'Yes sir'.

'Let the records show that Emily Hanson officially remains *missing, presumed dead.*

The defendant was sentenced to 12 years' imprisonment. No parole for 10 years.

As he was led away, handcuffed, the newly-convicted criminal shouted final words to the judge and jury.

'I didn't kill my wife. I have no idea what happened to her'.

The jurors stared back in silence.

The Judge assembled his papers and prepared for the next case.

CHAPTER 9   First day in prison

Wednesday 30th May 2012

Michael Hanson was led away and driven to Goa Prison where he was taken to a room to wait the arrival of a prison doctor.

The room had no windows and just one door.

The paint on the walls was peeling and the room resembled that of a doctor's examination room.

A couch with a screen around it, two chairs and a sink with taps that could be operated with an elbow.

In the corner of the room was a small table on which there was an open box of latex gloves, a stethoscope and Kleenex-branded tissues.

Next to the table was a set of old-fashioned scales, with sliding weights.

His mind was still reeling from the day's events and it wasn't over yet.

The doctor was there to create a record of his health, medication and notes of his general wellbeing on his first day in prison.

The last time Michael Hanson had had such a thorough examination was the obligatory company medical required by a health insurance company. This he suspected, would be different. The prison doctor wasn't working for his employer.

The doctor was accompanied by a male prison officer in uniform.

The officer sat on one of the chairs and watched as the doctor carried out the examination.

The doctor pronounced him to be in good health. 'A few pounds' overweight but nothing to worry about'. The prison diet would soon sort that out he thought.

The doctor's notes would be kept under lock and key in a four draw filing cabinet, for future reference.

He left the room and the prison officer took over.

After gesturing the prisoner to get dressed and take a seat the officer opened a briefcase and took out a copy of a 14-page document headed Goa Prison Rules.

He pushed it across the table towards the newly arrived prisoner.

Michael Hanson caught sight of one of the paragraphs that referred to work and a wage. It meant nothing to him. He was still trying to come to terms with what was happening.

He wasn't thinking straight. His mind ran riot as he tried to make sense of the day's events.

A sentence of 12 years meant he would be in prison until 2024.

As the prison officer went through a check list and basic rules, his new prisoner sat in silence and asked himself questions.

What would he look like in 2024?

What would the world look like?

Would anybody remember him?

Would there be anybody on the outside waiting to renew an old acquaintance or befriend him?

Bizarrely, he briefly wondered about his pension.

Do convicts get a pension, or do they forfeit the right as part of the punishment?

The officer ran through a well-rehearsed first day at school welcome speech.

There was a prison library. Michael Hanson briefly wondered if the shelves would hold any English language books or would he be expected to learn Hindu or Urdu or whatever the local language was.

The prison officer carried on going through his check list and explained that all prisoners were allowed to write four letters a month. Two at their cost and two at the Government's cost.

There would be no restriction on the number of incoming letters. All letters however, would be censored.

Visitors were allowed once a week and for no longer than 30 minutes.

The prison officer went on:

'Your prison number is 5940. From now on you will be known only as 5940.

The '5' prefix indicates to staff and other inmates that you are a Category 2 prisoner. It means you've been a bad boy. Anyone sentenced to 10 or more years is a CAT2.

'You'll soon get used to the language and the abbreviations.

CAT2 inmates will tell you that the only crime they committed was getting caught.

We are seriously overcrowded. All prisons throughout India are overcrowded.

You will be sharing a cell with two other CAT2 inmates.

I prefer to use the term inmate rather than prisoner'.

He continued:

'There are things you need to know that you won't find in the Rule Book.

Everybody here looks forward to new arrivals. It breaks the monotony.

As a relatively young man you will be of particular interest to some inmates.

One of your cellmates is looking for a new partner'.

'Partner? I'm not gay for Christ's sake!' snapped 5940.

'Neither was he when he arrived. Five years can change people. Anyway, I'm just drawing your attention to it'.

Nobody seemed to care that Prisoner 5940 had already lost his wife and now his own life was being taken away from him.

He would soon learn that life in prison was hard, and more so for a foreigner. It was always hot, sometimes unbearably hot, but not to everybody.

Most of the prisoners had grown up in India and were accustomed to the heat and humidity.

'Mosquitos' said the officer.

'Mosquitos! What about them?' answered the prisoner.

'They'll be waiting for you. Westerners smell differently to us. They appear like moths round a flame.

Mosquitoes are attracted to and guided by smell.

You will be given a month's supply of malaria tablets to get you past the worst. After that, if you want more, you'll need to see the doctor.

After a month of prison food your body odour will change and you'll begin to smell like the rest of us'.

The gay cellmate left him alone. He never worked out why, nor did he care. He was just thankful for small mercies.

It turned out that the third cellmate was a hardened criminal with no scruples or remorse whatsoever.

He was in jail for life for killing two people in broad daylight. He couldn't remember what prompted him to do it.

He said it could have been the way they looked at him.

It happened a long time ago and his memory had faded. The two unfortunate strangers who had caused him to lose his temper, were in the wrong place at the wrong time and paid for it with their lives. That was all he could remember. No hint of remorse.

5921 took a liking to 5940 and over the next few months a bizarre friendship developed.

One day in the dining hall, another CAT2 prisoner bumped into 5940. By accident or design nobody knew. In the seconds that followed 5921 jumped up, threw his plate of food on the floor and proceeded to launch an attack on the other inmate. He hit the concrete and felt the full force of a size 10 boot on the side of his head.

Before he had time to get up, his right arm was yanked upwards and smashed against the table, breaking at least two fingers. The crunch of breaking fingers caused cries of 'whoa' from everybody within earshot. The pain was excruciating.

Two guards arrived from nowhere, and 5921 was handcuffed and led away.

The prisoner with the damaged hand was accompanied by a third guard, and taken away from the dining hall through a different exit.

Later that day, after 5921 returned to the cramped cell to be greeted with a furious 5940. 'What did you think you were doing? That was completely unnecessary. You know you'll be be punished for what you did'.

'Hell, I'm already serving life. What are they going to do, add a few years?

Take away my privileges? Take away my library card?' mused the cellmate.

'They could take away your oils and paint brushes'.

5921's jaw dropped. He hadn't thought of that. That would be the worst punishment imaginable.

He loved to paint and over the years, had developed his ability and talent to become an accomplished artist.

'I'll speak up for you. I'll explain that you were only trying to help me, but in future, I'd prefer it if you'd leave me to sort out my affairs for myself'.

He didn't respond. He was thinking about his paintings. One wall of the shared cell was all but covered in his oil paintings.

The next day he was stripped, not just of his beloved oils and brushes, but all privileges for six months.

The paintings that had adorned the cell walls were removed and destroyed.

Another CAT2 inmate came from similar stock. He too had a short fuse and a ferocious temper. He took an instant liking to prisoner 5940 after he asked about his interest in books on fishing.

Amongst fellow inmates he was known as Vinny the Fly.

At 6' 5"and weighing 250 pounds he was somebody you'd definitely want on your side in a fight.

Vinny would spend all his spare time in the prison library reading books on fly fishing.

'When I get out I'm gonna spend the rest of my life in a boat on a lake', he would say.

When it came to all matters relating to fishing, he had an encyclopaedic memory. He knew all there was to know about fishing rods, dry flies, wet flies, buzzers and nymphs. He could argue tirelessly the relative merits of slow and rapid sinking lines.

Vinny lived in supreme hope. He had just four years to go and he would then be free to fish to his heart's content.

In all his time in prison, 5940 only came across one other inmate from the United Kingdom.

Prisoner 3114 came from Whittleford, a small village on the outskirts of Cambridge.

His PIN (Prison Identity Number) gave out the message that he was not considered to be a threat. He had been sentenced to 18 months for attempting to defraud a charity.

Prisoner 3114 was quite open and forthcoming about it. In fact, he was quite proud of himself.

He had been working in a children's charity in Mumbai when he stumbled across an opportunity to make easy money without affecting the charity.

Well, that's what he claimed in court but the magistrate didn't agree. Neither was he impressed with the mitigating circumstances when the accused pointed a finger of suspicion at the charity's internal accountant.

The prisoner claimed that he could prove that the accountant had been using creative accounting techniques to show that the charity was being well managed.

To an uninterested magistrate he tried to explain the ROA (Return on Assets) formula.

To 3114 it was obvious. To the magistrate it was irrelevant.

 The prisoner was sent down for 18 months.

The accountant carried on as before.

CHAPTER 10

Two years into a twelve stretch

Monday 12th May 2014

The first two years in prison passed slowly.

Every prisoner facing the prospect of a lengthy jail sentence, especially lifers, clutch at the very thought of freedom. Hope was ever present.

Without hope there was nothing to look forward to.

The parents of 5940 had both passed away. His wife was missing presumed dead. There were no children from the marriage and no siblings.

Most people could look forward to catching up with friends and family when they got out, but not Michael Hanson. He had neither friends nor family.

Anybody, known only by a four-digit number could die tomorrow and nobody would shed a tear.

He sometimes wondered how many people would attend his funeral.

Maybe a representative from the prison staff and a couple of inmates chained together at the ankles.

Not much to look forward to. In fact, he was losing the motivation he once had for getting out of prison.

Was this what was meant by becoming institutionalised?

He had seen the film Shawshank Redemption.

In the film, one prisoner, after being released from a long spell inside, committed a crime with the deliberate intention of being caught so that he could 'go home' as he put it.

How long he wondered, does it take to reach a point when it all becomes routine, and one stops fighting it.

Today would be like yesterday and tomorrow would be like today, and so it would go on. He'd been told by prisoners and prison staff, that eventually the boredom would be replaced by the comfort from knowing exactly what the next day would bring.

Weekends were no different to week days. Up at 5:00am. Lights out and lock down at 9.00pm.

As time went by he noticed how some inmates, who, in the outside world had nothing in common, began to develop strong friendships.

Strange friendships with unusual parings. Bankers formed friendships with bank robbers. Embezzlers bonded with accountants.

In a few cases heterosexuals formed intimate relationships with homosexuals.

Prison life threw people together in a way that would never happen on the outside.

5940 was thankful that he remained a fully signed up member of the 'straight club'.

He was grateful too that the food and diet was varied but wasn't keen on the strictly portion-controlled meals. He was used to big meals in America.

The prison guidelines in the prison rule book, which he'd read from beginning to end, were strictly adhered to: 2,400 calories a day for a male prisoner. 2,100 for a female. No second helpings.

As time passed by he worked in the prison kitchen. Washing pots and pans but, no knives and forks of course.

He discovered to his surprise that washing up could be therapeutic. A task that always starts out messy and ends up sparkling clean.

He learned to sew and was rewarded for his efforts by being paid a meagre wage. He turned scraps of material into floor mops.

In two years he reckoned he'd produced around 8000 mop heads.

Somewhere outside the prison a free man would be employed to secure the mop head to a long wooden handle. Too risky to allow prisoners to be given a wooden pole. It could be used as a weapon.

His hand-made mops were on sale at street markets from Delhi to Mumbai and beyond. He was helping to boost the Indian economy!

Looking on the positive side was a skill he learned from an English management consultant on a training programme called Thinking for Success.

The course leader was David Fossey aka Smiley.

He had the uncanny ability to turn any negative thought or statement into a positive one.

He would fine his students if they said anything negative. Money would go into a Sin Bin and handed over to a charity at the end of the course. He even persuaded people to pay up when they admitted to having a negative thought.

As a tribute to the tutor, and a reminder to himself, 5940 hung a hand-made sign with the words: Never, never, never, give up.

Fossey claimed the words were from Winston Churchill's shortest ever recorded speech.

5940 was full of fascinating quotes. It came from his love of English literature.

His gay cellmate continued to find new partners.

In the early days of his time behind bars, Michael Hanson often wondered if he'd ever hear from his wife again.

On the second anniversary of her disappearance he resigned himself to the fact that in all probability she was indeed 'missing presumed dead', and that he would never know the truth.

As he lay on his mattress in a hot, airless prison cell, Michael Hanson began to smile at the irony of it all.

He recalled how two years earlier he had told the judge that he and his wife had travelled to India to get away from the stresses of everyday life and have time to relax and unwind. He'd certainly had that wish granted. He wanted two weeks. The judge gave him 12 years.

He was reminded of Jeffrey Archer's book: Be Careful What You Wish For.

As he lay there, he was struck by another thought.

Six thousand miles away in Los Angeles was a law firm, McCartney, McCartney and Schumaker. The name sounded expensive and it was. All of their clients were rich. One had to be rich to be able to afford their exorbitant fees.

Theirs was not a 9 to 5 organisation. All employees were expected to work whatever hours it took to meet client deadlines. He knew that from first-hand experience. Prior to their trip to India, his wife had worked for the organisation for four years.

When asked by friends what her firm did, she would explain that they were involved in wealth management.

The firm's television and press advertising always included the words: 'Dedicated to look after you and your money - in the strictest confidence.'

In truth, the client base comprised rich and mega rich individuals who wanted to keep their wealth hidden and out of reach of the taxman.

This was done by setting up a company or trust in an offshore tax haven, typically located in the Cayman Islands, Bahamas, Panama, Monaco or the British Virgin Islands. There was a wide choice.

Clients could hang on to their money without breaking the law, by the clever use of little known legal loopholes.

Around the world, there are harbours and marinas with luxury yachts tied to their moorings, awaiting the periodic arrival of an owner.

This was the world his wife worked in and had intimate knowledge of.

Hanson couldn't help comparing the lives of convicted criminals in Goa prison, who may, once, have given into temptation, with the lives of the wealthy clients of McCartney, McCartney and Schumaker.

Clients who would never see the inside of a prison.

Clients who would never sleep in an overcrowded cell.

Clients who enjoyed all that money could buy and not have to worry about being interrogated or challenged about it.

A life of excess, where fine wines and vintage champagne were ever present.

His wife's rapid rise to stardom was due to hard work and long hours. She often worked into the early hours to make sure that clients could stay one step ahead of the law.

Her attention to detail, and acute awareness of the thin line that separates tax avoidance from tax evasion, marked her out for early promotion.

In private, she had been known to say that the world was full of bad crooks and good crooks. Bad crooks go to prison. Good crooks go to McCartney, McCartney and Schumaker.

She developed a hard exterior and was a tough negotiator. She would argue her point until she won the argument or the other party gave in. She always had to have the last word.

Time to reflect on his marriage brought into sharp focus the changes in his wife.

In the early days, fresh from law school, she stood up for justice and hated injustice. Later, she would argue that the real injustices in life were ill-conceived tax laws that metaphorically put handcuffs on entrepreneurs.

She saw her role as that of a facilitator.

As long as there were countries prepared to offer her clients anonymity, a safe haven and the obligatory safety deposit box, her firm would flourish. The obscenely high fees they charged for their services was never an issue.

His mind drifted to thoughts of Monica, their neighbour.

At college she excelled in sport and was an enthusiastic cheerleader.

She was captain of the college netball team and played in goal for the soccer team. She was a member of the 4 x 4 relay team, preferring to be a team player, rather than compete as an individual.

After college, and a brief spell as a sports coach, she married her High School sweetheart Geoff. They went on to adopt two children, having tried unsuccessfully to have children of their own.

There was nothing not to like about Monica or her husband. They were devoted to each other and their children, and were great friends and neighbours.

As his mind went over the events of life before prison, he began to wonder why a team player like Monica should suddenly have become interested in taking up golf. Golf is an individual sport. She'd asked him on more than one occasion if he'd be kind enough to put her name forward for membership at his golf club. At the time he thought nothing of it. It was no more than a friend asking a friend for a favour.

As he went over it in his mind the thought occurred to him that perhaps Monica had had an ulterior motive. Was is possible that she had feelings for him that he'd not picked up on? Was it in any way connected to the coolness and change in his wife's attitude?

It never occurred to him that it was anything more than a genuine desire to take up golf. With time to reflect, he began to question her motive and wonder if she had had a hidden agenda.

As he lay there he knew that he would probably never know the answer.

The questions kept coming. Could it be that she'd sent him signals which he'd not picked up on?

Had she liked him more than she'd let on?

What if? What if Emily had wrongly suspected something and kept quiet about it?

No, that didn't make sense. As he mulled it over in his mind he was closer to the truth than he realised. He dismissed the idea and put it down to a prison fantasy which he'd be warned about. Other inmates had warned him that the longer he stayed in prison the more likely it was that his mind would play tricks on him and he would confuse fact with fiction.

The fact was that Monica did have feelings for him.

The fact was that as visits to the golf club became more frequent, Emily's suspicions grew.

The fact was that Emily had her own hidden agenda. She secretly went about putting together a fool proof plan to teach them both a lesson. Her objective was that neither would connect their affair with what followed.

Long after Michael had gone to India and Emily had been declared missing presumed dead, Monica became consumed with guilt. Guilt in the knowledge that she had been willing to have an affair with Michael. Worse still, that she had been prepared to risk everything for something that could only result in disaster. She would have been cast as a marriage wrecker and lives would have been destroyed.

By the time Monica had decided to approach Emily about it, it was too late.

The memorial service had been held.

CHAPTER 11   A glimmer of hope

Monday 12th May 2014

Two years into his sentence, a mysterious letter arrived.

The letter was dated 22nd April 2014 but wasn't handed to him until Monday 12th May 2014.

The envelope had been opened and re-sealed.

He studied the envelope and saw that it was addressed to Michael J Hanson, Prisoner 5940, c/o HM Prison, Goa, India.

It was from an American lawyer working out of a small office in Green Bay, Wisconsin.

A town famed for having a population of 100,000 and a football stadium with the same capacity.

The letter began:

Dear 5940, (His name had been crossed out and replaced by his prison number) as if to remind him of his status in life and prison rules.

I am writing to introduce myself and inform you that over the next weeks and months I will write to you on a regular basis. My name is Richard Dadson, an American lawyer specialising in human rights issues.

I have accepted instructions to do all I can to have your case reviewed with the aim of getting a re-trial. My client wishes to remain anonymous. Even I do not know his or her identity.

As a gesture, and mark of good faith, the person(s) involved wishes you to know that they have deposited $50,000 dollars in my company's bank account. It is to be used for the sole purpose of having your case re-examined.

I have no plans to visit you at this stage but may do so in the future.

I urge you not to raise your hopes too high. In my experience these investigations can take months or even years with no guarantee of success.

I am being perfectly honest with you and must ask for the same in return,

My knowledge of your case is only what I know from a newspaper article sent to me by your anonymous benefactor.

From a two paragraph article published in the Los Angeles Times on 1st March 2014 I understand that in the Spring of 2012 you were in India and charged with the murder of your wife.

I write this on 22nd April 2014, which, by my reckoning, means you have already served two years of a 12-year sentence. Is that correct?

My understanding is that the case against you was based largely on circumstantial evidence. Is that correct?

Please remember that you are restricted to writing four letters per month. There is no restriction on the number of letters you may receive. All letters will be censored.

The Prison Superintendent has the right to withdraw permission at any time, and without explanation.

Over the coming weeks you need to provide me with honest answers to all my questions. I will do likewise.

If I am to be successful in having your case re-examined, you must send me everything I request.

I am communicating with the Supreme Court of India and have applied for a Special Leave to Appeal.

I look forward to hearing from you soon.

Yours,

Richard Dadson

Prisoner 5940's immediate thought was that it was a hoax. A sick joke.

He took it to the prison Superintendent who said that before handing it over he had already checked it out.

He was satisfied it was authentic. It was a genuine letter from a genuine lawyer.

The Superintendent explained that he had contacted the American Bar Association and had received written confirmation that Richard Dadson was a registered lawyer, practising in the State of Wisconsin.

The wheels of freedom were beginning to turn, albeit slowly.

The letter was already three weeks old.

CHAPTER 12   Early release
Friday 22nd May 2015 – Goa prison

From the time Dadson first took on the case, 5940 had spent two years behind bars.

It then took another seven months for the slow wheels of justice to come finally to a halt.

The decision by the Indian Supreme Court to overturn the original verdict guaranteed freedom for prisoner 5940.

It later transpired that outside forces were working in the background had an impact on the decision.

The examination of the trial transcript papers supported Dadson's claim of bias by the police, whose case rested almost entirely on hearsay and circumstantial evidence.

When the case came to court the transcript showed that the jury had been misdirected by the persuasive prosecutor, but most important, Dadson produced evidence that the police had failed to file the prosecution papers by the due date. That alone would surely have been enough, but Dadson was the consummate professional.

He raised the case with the Supreme Court in India; the British Foreign Office in London and the European Court of Human Rights in Strasbourg.

For an individual to have such influence on so many departments was unprecedented.

Time honoured guiding principles of 'innocent until proven guilty' and 'beyond reasonable doubt' sealed the case in favour of his client.

Notwithstanding the above, Dadson cautioned the Foreign Office of an international outcry should he take the story to the British press.

He enclosed a copy of the popular Daily Mail with an article headed:

Indian Foreign Aid Scandal.

The UK is to give India another quarter of a billion pounds in aid by 2019 - the same amount New Delhi spent to launch its first mission to put a man on the moon.

With an election coming up in the spring, Dadson knew that the British media could use this story and influence the outcome.

The polls were saying that the result was too close to call. It could go either way.

David Cameron was fighting to remain Prime Minister and Ed Miliband; the leader of the Opposition was snapping at his heels.

Negative publicity had to be avoided at all costs.

The Conservative party couldn't afford to have their foreign aid programme ridiculed any more than it was. They needed closure and fast.

Dadson added fuel to the fire by announcing that he was ready to expose further injustice, pointing out that a

British citizen had already spent two years behind bars on a trumped up charge.

A British citizen 'had been left to languish in an overcrowded, rat-infested jail'. He knew the press would pick up on that. It would make a huge human interest story. It had potential to run and severely damage the reputations of politicians seeking re-election.

In the world of International politics, a simple phone call from one Ambassador to another can be enough to change the course of history.

The best that Dadson and his client could have hoped for was for a re-trial.

What they got was a full pardon plus an unprecedented amount in compensation.

Six million dollars would make his client a rich man.

The prison authorities in Goa were instructed to prepare release papers for prisoner 5940.

Michael Hanson would shortly be a free man.

CHAPTER 13   The strangers meet

Sunday 24th May 2015.

Departure lounge – Heathrow Airport

This was the day when Prisoner 5940 would make use of his PIN (*prison* identity number) and use it to make a credit card purchase.

5940 had been chosen by his lawyer for his new PIN (*personal* identity number).

He didn't need permission to go shopping, sit in a coffee shop or restaurant and could eat or drink whenever, and wherever he liked.

The freedom he'd dreamed of for years, felt unnatural at first. It was going to take time to get used to.

As he walked among other passengers he marvelled at the sight of people using laptops, mobile phones and devices he didn't recognise.

People of all ages and nationalities mingled and jostled in virtual silence.

Each one of them waiting to hear that their flight was being called and ready for boarding.

In most cases, the only information a passenger needed was displayed on the departure board.

Multiple pairs of eyes scanned the digital information boards which were continually updated. Eyes searched for flight number, then boarding gate and time of departure, all the time hoping not to see the word 'delayed'.

In addition to the visual display, an anonymous voice made announcements over the airport speaker system to alert passengers that their flight was 'now boarding'.

That was the trigger to gather up belongings and move swiftly to the departure gate.

As seats near the departure board were vacated, they were immediately taken by new passengers and the cycle would start all over. Flight number, boarding gate, time of departure.

The heightened security at airports required all passengers to arrive at least two hours before departure. Inevitably, this led to hundreds of people milling around with time to kill.

Some would sit quietly, read a book, use the time to catch up on emails or phone messages or work silently on their tablet or laptop. Armies of fingers surfing miniature keyboards to send a never-ending stream of emails and text messages.

Passenger 5B had never sent a text in his life. He planned to use his time on the flight to learn how to use his new mobile phone. He hoped 12 hours would be enough.

Every seat in every café, coffee shop or bar was taken. There were always more passengers than seats. The moment one became available there was a frantic scramble to claim it.

Passenger 5B watched and noted the behaviour of fellow passengers. Some who had clearly finished their food and drink were reluctant to give up their seat in case the seats on the outside had already been taken.

He made his way to the duty free shop. A female passenger, who would soon play a major part in his life, was already in line, a few paces ahead of him, neither aware of the other.

She was holding a wire basket carrying a magazine and perfume.

There were just two items in his basket. A book by Jeffrey Archer on his life in prison, and Nelson Mandela's autobiography. As he stood in line, he looked down at his newly acquired unused pay-as-you-go mobile phone and wondered how many numbers he'd have to put in the electronic phone book. Not many to begin with.

As they approached the checkout they both reached for a passport and boarding card. The female passenger was holding a boarding card with the number 5A.

The male passenger was holding an almost identical one with the number 5B.

Soon the two numbers would place them together where they would sit, side-by-side for the long journey home.

Two strangers destined to meet on a plane.

They independently checked the departure board. Flight NZ001 was 'now boarding'.

They edged forwards, anxious to pay for their goods and head towards the boarding gate.

As passenger 5B paid for his purchases he allowed himself a rueful smile as he tapped in his PIN number, slowly and deliberately...5 9 4 0. His old prisoner identity number was now his personal identity number.

Starting today, every time he paid for goods with plastic, his secret PIN number would serve as a reminder of life behind bars.

The time in England was 16:00 local time. The time in Los Angeles was 08:00. Airports favour the 24-hour clock to avoid the problem of passengers turning up 12 hours early or 12 hours late.

Michael Hanson was more used to the 12-hour time clock he'd become accustomed to in prison.

It was 4:00pm in England and 8:00am in Los Angeles. Same day and date. Two cities separated by 6000 miles and eight hours.

Many of the residents of Los Angeles would already be on their way to work and dealing with rush hour traffic.

He remembered how frustrating it was when, years before, he would switch lanes to join one that was moving faster, only to find it was the wrong decision. Cars that had been behind a few moments earlier would soon be passing and gaining ground.

The two strangers took their seats. Air New Zealand flight NZ001 was due to depart on schedule at 16:15.

As the flight crew went through pre-flight checks, cabin staff distributed head-sets, pillows and blankets and prepared to welcome new passengers on board. Some passengers had started their journey 12 hours before in Auckland. Their journey would last 24 hours.

It was little wonder that most appeared to be drowsy or asleep.

A flight attendant walked through the cabin with an aerosol can. Foreign airborne bugs were not welcome in America.

Flight time to Los Angeles was expected to be 11 hours and 20 minutes.

Passenger 5A was relieved to see her fellow passenger 5B pre-occupied with the inflight magazine and checking out the list of films. She was unaware that the last time he'd seen a film of his choice was three years ago in a beach-front hotel in Goa, India.

For the last three years he had watched countless Bollywood style films. Lots of beautiful people falling in love, non-stop smiling and dancing and always came with a happy ending, typical of the closing scene of Slumdog Millionaire.

At least the dialogue of the Oscar winning Slumdog Millionaire was in English. Most of the others came with English sub-titles. Seventeen spoken Indian words translated into five English words that disappeared from the screen after three seconds. 5B soon acquired rapid reading skills.

Two hours into the flight neither passenger had struck up conversation.

A flight attendant arrived with a hot meal. The choice of chicken or beef. They both ordered the chicken.

As the journey continued he began to read Nelson Mandela's book A Long Walk to Freedom.

5A opened her tablet. 5B glanced down and was amazed to see how small it was.

He had never before seen such a small computer.

5A became aware of his interest.

'Is that a computer?' He'd broken the ice.

They started a conversation with him doing most of the talking. She was a good listener. They talked non-stop for almost four hours as he shared his life with a stranger on a plane.

As he opened up he shared his life's trials and tribulations and felt a sense of relief.

He wasn't looking for conversation. Just somebody willing to listen. It didn't matter if she was interested.

All that mattered was that she appeared to listen and if she really was interested that would be a bonus.

As he continued to speak 5A continued to listen and listened in awe. She was the first person he'd spoken to in years who didn't seem to have an ulterior motive or angle, as his inmates would call it.

You can't trust anybody on the outside was their mantra.

Apart from Dadson, his American lawyer, a gay cellmate and hardened criminals locked up in an Indian jail, he hadn't found anybody willing to listen to him for years. 5A was a breath of fresh air.

Whenever he paused to take a breath 5A stepped in.

She asked lots of questions. She was like a talk-show host. She asked lots of open questions that forced her fellow passenger to elaborate.

Soon she knew his life story but her life to him was an unknown quantity. He knew she preferred chicken to beef but not much more. He wasn't even aware that she hadn't told him her name.

Having a conversation suggests two-way communication. This was one way. He talked, she listened.

The last female who had shown any interest in what he had to say was his wife, but that was more than three years ago.

5A continued to ask questions and 5B voluntarily furnished the answers.

The more she listened the more animated he became.

She became spellbound by the story of his trial, life in prison, encounters with hardened criminals and sudden release.

From time to time the flight attendant would walk through the cabin with a drinks trolley.

5A interrupted: 'Were you allowed alcohol in prison?'
She immediately realised it was a dumb question.

'That's alright', he replied. 'You soon find out that it's OK to kill yourself with the freely available drugs and cigarettes, but not alcohol. Everybody in prison is teetotal.

'What are your plans when you get home?'

'First priority is to check if Dadson has sold the house. I've already appointed him as my lawyer.

I wrote that I had no desire to return to my old house and old way of life. He could put the furniture in store'.

He said he was planning to hire Dadson to establish what really happened to his wife.

He had the money to hire a private detective and needed answers to a number of questions:

Did she remain in India?

Was she killed?

Was someone else involved?

Whatever the outcome, he needed to know so he could put the matter to rest and get on with rebuilding his life.

The second priority was to track down and meet his benefactor.

What 5B didn't know was that his home had already been sold to a property developer. His bank account had been emptied and he had no other assets.

His erstwhile wife was alive and well and had all sorts of surprises waiting in store.

As they approached Los Angeles 5A was running out of time and needed to know more.

Her journalistic instincts kicked in.

'Maybe I can help? asked 5A.

'I don't think so' replied 5B.

'Where are you staying in LA?' she asked.

'I was planning to check in at the Hilton Hotel at the airport. I have the money'.

She thought for a brief moment that she might invite him to stay at her apartment, but changed her mind.

He was good looking and hadn't slept with a woman for three years. She put that to the back of her mind.

'I plan to get a taxi home'.

She offered to drop him off at the hotel.

'I can drop you off at the hotel if you like. The Hilton is on my way home'.

'How about tomorrow? How about me joining you tomorrow morning for breakfast? My treat. There's somebody I'd like you to meet'.

'Who?' he replied.

'Ah, that's for me to know and you to find out' she said with a smile.

Here, this is my phone number'.

He thought it odd that she didn't hand him a business card. She surely must have one. It was the boarding card for seat 5A with her number written on it.

She suggested that once through customs they could meet outside the terminal by the taxi rank.

She explained that they would have to line up in separate channels to clear customs.

As a British citizen he would have to go to the channel marked Aliens. She would head for one marked US Citizens.

Before he had time to answer and with ten minutes before landing, 5A excused herself and went to the bathroom.

She never returned to her seat.

5B assumed that she'd had enough of his company and needed a break. He wouldn't blame her. After all he'd been talking non-stop for the best part of 4-5 hours.

He guessed she was probably sitting in another row, head down, trying hard not to be seen.

A few minutes earlier she seemed keen to meet again. Maybe she'd changed her mind.

When the aircraft came to a standstill, passengers reached up to the overhead locker, grabbed their belongings and moved slowly along the aisle and waited while the exit doors were unlatched and opened.

Passenger 5B remained in his seat. He wasn't in a hurry. He stayed there until everybody else had left the aircraft.

He watched in case he saw 5A making her way to the exit. No sign of her. She must have slipped past him and gone on ahead.

He last saw her heading towards a lavatory. As he walked past, he pushed the door open. It was empty. Nobody there. He carried on walking, glancing occasionally over his shoulder, but the aisles were empty. When he reached the exit he acknowledged the smiling stewardess with a nod and a thank you.

He made his way down the steps of the 747 and joined the queue of fellow passengers heading towards immigration. He wondered who it was who decided that Aliens was a good signage choice. Why not something a little friendlier and welcoming like Visitors or Foreigners. Anything but Aliens.

It took an hour to get through customs. As he arrived at passport control he was asked to stare into a camera so that his eyeballs could be photographed. What was that all about?

He passed through passport control. Didn't see any aliens. Suddenly, in front of him in the next line, just below the US Citizens sign, was something that caught his attention.

A woman in a raincoat and sunglasses was being questioned by the customs official at passport control. She removed her sunglasses and the official instantly recognised her, smiled and waved her through. 5B didn't give it another thought.

He proceeded towards the taxi rank. The invitation to share a taxi and meet up later was obviously a ploy. He was a tad disappointed. He couldn't help feeling he'd been let down, albeit gently, but decided it was probably no more than he deserved. He had, after all given her a bit of an ear bashing.

Just then, the lady in the raincoat and sunglasses smiled and beckoned him over. It was 5A. No longer a blonde with short hair. She was a brunette with shoulder-length hair.

'Come with me'. Without stopping to explain, she grabbed his hand and dragged him to a waiting taxi as the passenger door opened automatically.

As 5A got in, the driver looked over his right shoulder, and with a broad grin said, 'It is you. I didn't recognise you at first.

I watched you earlier on the news channel. Outside Buckingham Palace'. She ignored him.

Once again 5A and 5B were sitting side by side as passengers, heading in the same direction.

Who is this lady? he thought. Why did she run away? Why had she tried to disguise herself?

Was she on the run?

He thought one thing and said another.

'You disappeared. What happened?'

'I'll explain later'.

The taxi drew up at the Hilton Hotel.

As he turned to get out, she kissed him lightly on the cheek. 'See you later'. she said, and with that the door closed automatically and the taxi drove off with 5A looking back, smiling and waving.

5B didn't have a reservation, but he knew that airport hotels were rarely full. This was no different.

He signed the register using the pen standing upright in a holder. The pen was embossed with the name of the hotel and attached to the stand with a string of silver coloured beads.

It felt good to sign the register under his own name.

He replaced the pen in its holder and glanced down at his signature then looked up to the smiling receptionist.

It felt good to be treated as an individual again.

A hotel porter appeared from nowhere and placed his luggage on an oversized luggage trolley. All he had was a parcel wrapped in brown paper, a plastic bag with two books, and an incongruous mop head.

The porter was polite and escorted him to his room.

The room was big. About three times bigger than his cell, and lavishly furnished.

It took ten strides to reach the dressing table, where he placed the mop head next to a vase of fresh flowers. He leant forward and held his nose over the brightly coloured blooms. As he smelt them he put his hand out to touch one of the petals. The flowers were real.

He looked around the room and spotted a door. He walked across and gently pushed it open.

The door swung silently open revealing another part of his new world.

He took one step inside, stopped, and stared.

He was greeted with more luxury.

The bathroom was larger even than the three-man cell in Goa. At least 50% larger.

Full length mirrors on the walls; two basins with gold taps and an upturned shell with Hilton Hotel soap.

In the reflection of one of the mirrors, he could see two white towelling bathrobes hanging from two gold hooks.

The robes were embroidered. He couldn't make out the reflected words but presumed they would be Hilton Hotel. The thick towelling robes served the dual purpose of comfort and deterrent.

Comfort for the guests. Deterrent for the hotel.

Guests had a habit of taking home hotel branded souvenirs.

He smiled. His old inmates wouldn't see that as a deterrent. They'd see it as an invitation.

His mind went back as he tried to picture his friends back in Goa standing in line to use a communal toilet. He felt sad but then he smiled again as he started to hum the lines from Shirley MacLaine's hit song from Sweet Charity came to him:

'If - they - could - see me now'. If only.

He walked back into the bedroom and caught sight of the mini bar. Another ten strides and he was there.

He opened the door and checked the contents.

Lined up on one of the two shelves was a selection of miniature bottles of spirit, with the obligatory Jack Daniels in the centre. He took out a cold can of Budweiser and a packet of salted peanuts.

There was an armchair in the room. He sat down. Pulled on the metal ring on top of the can and enjoyed the sound of the air being released, and watched as the bubbles appeared as froth.

Next, he picked up the remote control and looked across at the biggest flat screen TV he'd ever seen. It was wall mounted.

He pressed the top button. The red standby light went out and on came a green light and then the whole screen lit up.

As his eyes adjusted to the brightness he saw a message.

Welcome Mr Michael J Hanson. We hope you enjoy your stay at the Hilton Hotel, Los Angeles.

The TV was pre-tuned to a 24-hour news channel.

He leaned back and began to sip the beer and then, suddenly, sat bolt upright!

5A was on the screen, alone, holding a microphone. She was outside Buckingham Palace in England.

Tens of thousands of people were lining the Mall just as a formation of World War II aircraft flew overhead.

5A had been in London to report on the celebration to mark the 70th anniversary of VE (Victory in Europe) day.

She never mentioned that.

The date on the screen was showing 8th May 2015. Two weeks ago.

For a moment he froze. Unable to take it all in. He stared. No doubt about it. It was her alright.

He watched intently. Gradually, it began to make sense. 5A was a television reporter with CNN. That was clear from the microphone she was holding.

He felt utterly betrayed. His fellow inmates had warned him not to trust anybody and here, staring right at him, from the 60" plasma screen, was living proof.

He'd been warned that everybody had an angle and she certainly did. His new found friend wasn't a friend at all. She was a scheming individual out to use him to get another story.

He took the stub of the boarding pass with her phone number on, and tore it into small pieces, dropping them one by one into the waste bin next to the armchair.

He guessed that the person she'd wanted him to meet was a colleague of maybe her boss. It didn't matter. He didn't care. As far as he was concerned they could go to hell.

CHAPTER 14   Hilton Hotel - Los Angeles

Monday 25th May 2015

5A sat at a table in the hotel dining room at a table set for breakfast for three. With her was her boss from CNN.

A waiter brought over a jug of coffee.

'What time did you say you'd meet?'

'8:30'.

They sat in silence.

'It's nine o'clock. Give him a call' he said impatiently.

'I don't have his number'.

'Well, get it from Reception.'

'I don't know his name'.

'What! Wait a minute. Let me get this straight. You sat with this guy for 12 hours on a plane. He tells you his whole fucking life story and you don't know his name? Is that what you're telling me?'

She stayed silent.

He raised his voice. Other hotel guests couldn't help overhearing. He couldn't have cared less. He was her boss and he was angry.

'Did you and 5 fucking B join the mile-high club? Is that it? Too busy to swap names but plenty of time for two strangers on a plane to have it off?'

'I'll ignore that remark'.

They sat in silence.

'You know what I think? I think he's not coming. I think he went to his room, turned on the goddam TV and saw you staring back at him. That's what I think. He probably saw you on last night's news.

Your 5B mystery man, knows exactly who you are and he won't show.

Trust me. Right now he's probably sitting in his room having breakfast wondering what the hell is going on'.

He was right. 5B was in his room having breakfast alone, watching CNN. He watched in case 5A re-appeared. He sat, watching, listening and thinking.

Back in the hotel dining room her boss continued to rant. 'Jeez. The Queen of England has stopped him from joining us for breakfast. You couldn't write this stuff'.

'OK. Here's what you're gonna do.

'First thing tomorrow, you go to Green Bay, Wisconsin and find this Dadson guy.

'Find out his name, 5 fucking B that is. His lawyer must know his name.

'Find out who he is and everything else you can. Things he didn't tell you on the plane.

Get a lead on the benefactor. Where do they live? What's their motive? Why are they prepared to spend what must be thousands of dollars on a complete stranger? What have they got to hide?'

'What if he won't co-operate?' she replied.

'Tell him he has a new client...CNN. That'll do the trick'.

As he walked away from the table he stopped, turned around and said; 'And another thing, last night on TV you said 24 degrees is hot. Here in America we use Fahrenheit. Please remember that. You're not in England any more'. He didn't wait for an answer. He was gone.

Next day was Tuesday 26th May 2015.

5A caught the first flight to Green Bay. Her secretary sent the address by text.

At 11:00am she was sitting in Dadson's office exchanging pleasantries when his mobile phone rang.

He glanced down at the screen and saw the number 5940. He made an apology. 'Excuse me. I need to take this.' and walked out of the office.

'I have CNN here. What's going on?' said an incredulous Dadson.

'I'm across the road in a coffee bar'. Dadson paused.

'OK. Leave it to me. Have another coffee. I'll call you when we're through'.

Twenty minutes later Michael Hanson's new phone rang. He got up, paid for two cups of coffee and a Danish and walked across the road to Dadson's office, carrying with him a large brown paper parcel. Inside was a framed picture.

Dadson watched him stride purposefully towards his office.

Dadson was not a bit like the person Hanson had in his head.

Dadson was waiting by the door of his office. Hand outstretched. He wore a broad smile.

The lawyer looked like Sean Connery in his sixties. Silver hair and a goatee beard.

They shook hands and then embraced. Like two old friends who hadn't seen each other for years.

Hanson asked: 'What did she want?'

'Whatever it was, she didn't get it.' and then with a broad smile said:

'I have a banker's draft for you.'

'I have something for you too', and with that he handed the parcel to Dadson who cut the string with a pair of scissors and gently pulled away the protective paper.

Inside was a framed picture. An oil painting of a prison cell in India. No wonder the Superintendent wanted to get rid of it.

Dadson then unfolded a piece of paper which had the words "Never, never, never give up". He recognised the handwriting from Michael Hanson's letters.

Michael Hanson spoke up: 'That message kept me going in prison. I'd like you to have that and the painting. They go together'.

He studied the painting and noticed in the bottom right hand corner, where one would normally find a signature, there was a four-digit number. 5940.

'I love it. I know exactly where I'll hang it'.

He pointed to a framed picture on the wall opposite his desk.

On it was a framed photograph of the Green Bay Packers, resplendent in their green and gold kit with a replica of the Super Bowl which they last won in 2011. He used Blue Tac to fix the handwritten message from Winston Churchill.

'Take note guys'.

CHAPTER 15 Memorial service

Thursday 18th October 2012

Six months after she went missing in India, the wife of prisoner 5940 attended her own memorial service, disguised as a guest.

She heard her Pastor speak fondly of her.

Hymns were sung. Prayers were said.

At the end of the service the small gathering of friends and neighbours drifted away and returned to their lives.

No family members attended. Emily Hanson's parents had passed away four years earlier and she and her husband had no children or siblings.

The announcement of the memorial service had been in the local newspaper a month earlier on 18th September 2012.

She fully expected to see her bereft husband in the crowd. He didn't show up.

He was washing dishes in Goa prison, still trying to come to terms with life as a convicted criminal.

He still had eleven and a half years to serve.

In planning her disappearance, Emily Hanson had estimated that she would need her husband to be detained in India helping police with their enquiries for five or six days.

She needed time to complete her check list of things to be done before he arrived home.

Unbeknown to Michael Hanson, his 'missing presumed dead' wife had put the house up for sale a week before they'd departed for India.

By the time they'd arrived in Goa, the house had been on the market for a week and attracted a lot of interest at the fire sale price.

She hadn't wanted to arouse his suspicions which was one of the reasons for not confronting him about his affair.

She'd already decided never take him back. She was intent on making the unsuspecting pair suffer.

In her scheming mind she would take pleasure in knowing they would suffer without understanding why. Mental torment designed to drive them crazy.

By her calculations she expected her husband would spend the first two to three days searching the hotel and surrounding area, before going to the police.

Knowing him as she did, she knew that never in his wildest dream would he think that she'd gone back to America, and never in *her* wildest dream did she imagine he'd gone to prison.

All she wanted was to make him suffer the indignity of being questioned by the police, before being allowed to go free.

Eventually, he would have to choose between staying on in India or returning home without her.

Whatever his decision, he couldn't win.

The longer he stayed in India, the better it would be for her.

By the time he returned home, he would find he had no home to return to, no wife and no money.

The final part of her plan to disappear off the face of the earth was to arrange her own memorial service.

All that was required was to place an announcement in the local newspaper and allow the word to spread.

Just in case an inquisitive husband or the police came looking for her, the search would end at the church.

Given a choice, she would have much preferred the announcement to have been of a funeral or cremation, but that was out of the question.

There was no body to bury. She was still using it.

She congratulated herself on devising a plan, worthy of the most elaborate Agatha Christie detective story, but Emily Hanson was no Agatha Christie. It was destined to go wrong, seriously wrong.

Out of the corner of her eye she saw a tearful Monica, dressed in black. Monica was the best friend who she thought, had an affair with her husband.

Monica was attending the service on her own. Her husband Geoff had died from cancer two years earlier.

Monica went back to her empty house, took out some writing paper and began to write:

Dear Emily,

My dear, dear, Emily, I am so sorry. I just don't know where to begin.

Why didn't I speak to you before? Why has it taken until now for me to tell you how I feel?

Call it a woman's instinct but I somehow knew you thought Michael and I had a thing going. We didn't.

I should have talked to you about it at the time, but decided not to in case I'd misread the signals. You would have been angry with me. Me, your best friend. I'd have felt utterly foolish, and hugely embarrassed, so I left it.

Now, you're dead and it's too late to put it right. You've gone from this earth, thinking only the worst of me.

I did love Michael, but not in the way you imagined. You loved my husband Geoff, just as Geoff loved you and Michael.

We had so many happy times together. We would tease Michael about his British accent, whilst secretly admiring him for it.

Michael would tease us about not being able to make a decent cup of tea.

Happy times. Four friends. Two families sharing one life.

Now I'm alone. Geoff battled with cancer for a long time and eventually gave up the fight.

I don't believe what the papers say about Michael and maybe nobody will ever know the truth of what happened in India.

A tear fell and splashed silently onto the paper.

She was too upset to sign the letter.

Monica stood up and walked slowly to the patio door, through which she could see the Weber barbecue with the black protective cover on, standing on a neatly trimmed lawn.

The two families had shared so many happy times together on that very spot.

She looked at the four canvas-covered chairs, wooden picnic table with a closed sun umbrella.

She went to the barbecue and took hold of the wooden handle, turning it gently in an anti-clockwise direction. Something that Geoff or Michael had always done in the past. Now it was down to her. She was the only one remaining out of a group of four.

The lid came away and she placed it on the ground. She never did quite master the knack of hanging it on the side.

She took the letter she'd just written, read it one more time, screwed it up into a ball and placed it on the black metal grill.

She lit a match and carefully set fire to the ball of paper and watched as the flames took hold.

The ball unfolded as it began to burn.

She stood back as the burnt pieces floated upwards towards heaven, towards Emily.

CHAPTER 16   Home alone

On the very same day that she was declared missing from her hotel in India, Emily Hanson was on her way home to America. It was Thursday 26th April 2012.

Over the weeks that followed she went about the second part of her elaborate plan.

She sold their home at a fire sale price, withdrew their joint life savings, and closed their joint bank account.

She then cashed in stocks and bonds.

Her total assets amounted to $1,600,000, give or take a few cents.

She was financially secure. It had been much easier than she thought.

She began to reflect on recent events.

She knew that her husband would eventually give up the search and return home. He would have no option. He could stay in India as long as he liked, weeks or months even, and still never find her.

That is when he would return to their marital home and come face-to-face with financial ruin.

Would he ever, she thought, make the connection between the affair with Monica and his own wife's disappearance?

She knew that police would check airports, bus and railway stations for any sightings.

She thought she'd thought about everything.

As things turned out, the disguise she wore as she left the hotel was unnecessary.

When the police came to check CCTV footage they discovered that the tapes had been accidentally wiped clean by a new member of staff.

She mentally congratulated herself on the success of her plan.

Disappearing without trace in a foreign country had also been easier than expected.

Leaving behind personal belongings like her mobile phone, laptop, purse, make-up bag and passport would convince the most cynical that she had to be somewhere in India. Where else could she be?

The phone she deliberately left behind was her old phone, complete with call history and contacts. She'd already copied all the numbers on to a new Sim card which was in her new phone.

She'd purchased that before travelling to India.

It was a short drive to the California/Nevada border where she paid for the new phone in cash.

The old phone was left in the hotel as a decoy.

Even if she called somebody with the new phone, by accident, it would show on their screen as an unknown number.

Getting a second passport was much easier than she imagined.

She'd heard that frequent flyers are sometimes issued with a second passport.

One to use on an oversea trip, and another to send to a foreign embassy when applying for an entry visa. That process could take weeks so a second passport, for well-seasoned travellers was essential.

All she had to do was download an application form and post it to the American Embassy in Los Angeles enclosing a pre-stamped and addressed envelope.

A new passport arrived two weeks later.

After the police became involved she knew that all eventualities would have to be exhausted before her husband would be allowed to return home.

She even imagined him going through a checklist. He was thorough. Adulterers knew how to cover their tracks. She knew he would leave no stone unturned.

Had she tripped and hit her head?

Was she wandering aimlessly in a foreign country suffering from amnesia?

Had she been abducted?

There would be interviews at the hotel, trips to the police station and surrounding area and numerous interviews.

She banked on him being believed and set free.

As her husband was heading for prison she carried on with her plan to leave the country undetected.

Arriving at passport control at Mumbai Airport, she had one final hurdle to overcome.

She waited nervously as the customs officer looked carefully at her passport.

He looked at the departing passenger and then at the photograph in the passport.

He glanced back and forth.

Emily Hanson was frozen to the spot.

After what seemed like an eternity, the customs officer slowly closed the passport and handed it over to an outstretched hand.

As she passed through the barrier the officer looked up, smiled and said:

'Enjoy your flight Miss da Gama'.

She always did prefer her maiden name.

CHAPTER 17   Bombshell

Emily Hanson casually browsed the local newspaper.

She paused when she saw the headline: "Englishman jailed for murder". At first it didn't register.

People get murdered every day in America.

Her eyes were about to move to another headline when she suddenly stopped.

Two words that leapt from the page: Goa, India. Two words that set her heart racing.

She sat down. Read and re-read the article several times.

She looked at the date on top of the newspaper. It was yesterday, Tuesday 9th October 2012.

In her mind she retraced events. She had flown back from India on 27th April 2012, six months before the article was printed.

Her mind raced. That would explain why her husband hadn't been at the memorial service or made any attempt to get in touch.

In his mind she was still missing and for all he knew she could be dead.

She scoured the article for more information. The couple were not named. The story referred to a middle-aged Englishman detained in prison on a murder charge.

The article went on. The victim was his American born wife. The body had not been found. The British husband had been jailed for 12 years.

'TWELVE YEARS?' she cried. 'Jailed for 12 years'.

Her mind raced, her pulse raced. From being calm and collected she was reduced to a gibbering wreck.

The newspaper was a day old but it referred to a trial held months earlier.

She tried to make sense of the dates. If it turned out that the person in jail was indeed her husband, he would already have spent six months in prison for a crime he hadn't committed. The real crime had gone undetected. The real crime was committed by her when she disappeared without a trace.

Only Emily Hanson knew the truth. She decided to act.

If she went to the police she'd be arrested and extradited to India to face trial herself.

There had to be another way.

That night she didn't go to bed. She sat in an armchair staring at the newspaper.

Over and over she muttered the words: 'Twelve years, twelve years'.

As the sun came up she had an outline of a plan.

She knew she had to find a way to get him out of prison, without anybody knowing she was alive.

Whatever she did had to be done in complete secret.

The plan had to be water tight and untraceable.

She decided that she would need to become an anonymous benefactor.

However much she hated him for what he'd done, he didn't deserve to be locked up behind bars, and certainly not on the other side of the world in a foreign country, especially for a crime that hadn't been committed.

She sat at a table, took a writing pad and pen and began to make a list of what had to be done.

- LAWYER. Engage a lawyer. One that had no previous contact or dealings with her or her husband.
- ANONYMOUS. Nobody must ever know who was paying the bills.
- LOCATION. The lawyer needed to be located in another state. Minimum 1000 miles away.
- TRACK RECORD. Somebody with experience of international human rights issues.

Having jotted down the basic requirements, she searched the internet. Before long she had the name of Richard Dadson. He met all the criteria and worked from an office in Green Bay, Wisconsin.

She wrote an introductory letter and mailed it using a PO Box as the return address.

Enclosed with the letter was a photocopy of a certified and as yet, unsigned cheque, for $50,000 made out to his law firm.

Richard Dadson smiled. This was an entirely new experience.

The terms and conditions and rules of engagement were in bullet point format.

- The money could only be used to further the cause of Michael Hanson's release.
- The client expected a weekly update in writing, posted to a PO Box.
- A breakdown of costs incurred plus hours worked to be sent monthly with an invoice.
- There would be no face-to-face meetings, no telephone contact, no text messages of email messages.
- No attempt to be made to identify the benefactor or their location.

Dadson was intrigued. He relished a challenge and this one came with an upfront payment of $50,000.

Richard Dadson accepted the assignment.

CHAPTER 18   5A visits Goa prison

Saturday 20th June 2015

A month after her abortive meeting with Dadson, 5A jetted off to Goa in an attempt to find out as much as she could about prisoner 5940's trial and life behind bars.

She knew that her boss was still furious. She didn't need to have it spelt out that her future with CNN rested on the success or failure of this assignment.

She was under no illusion that she had to come back with an exclusive, and enough material for her boss to release daily snippets of information to keep the story running for at least a week.

The long journey started in Los Angeles and took her via London and Mumbai to a coastal resort in Goa, where she'd arranged to meet prison Superintendent Patel.

She booked into the same hotel that the Hanson's stayed at three years before.

After a good night's sleep, she walked through the hotel lobby and out to the pool area where she busied herself taking photographs. Nobody took any notice. It was an everyday occurrence.

At 10:00am a taxi collected her from the hotel entrance and took her to her appointment with the prison Superintendent at Goa Prison.

After a brief security check, she was ushered into a large, air-conditioned office. The centre piece was a highly polished mahogany desk with three chairs lined up in front, ready for an interview or interrogation.

Prisoners were never invited to sit down.

They stood, handcuffed with their hands behind their backs facing the Superintendent.

On this occasion, the Superintendent had cleared his desk and cancelled all other appointments so that he could give his full attention to the VIP guest.

He had never appeared on television before.

This would be his debut interview with the world famous CNN news channel and he was determined that it should go without a hitch.

The Superintendent had a reputation for being a hard but fair task master.

Punishment for minor offences was swift and effective. Immediate withdrawal of privileges, confiscation of personal belongings and eating meals alone.

More serious offences led to immediate spells in solitary confinement with one hour a day for exercise in the prison yard... after all other prisoners had been locked up for the night.

Everybody throughout the prison, from senior to junior staff and all inmates had been warned to be on their best behaviour, or face the consequences.

5A was given a tour of the prison and invited to meet the prisoners who shared the same cell as 5940.

The television audience would see mutual respect, efficiency and firmness.

For the VIP, no place in the prison would be out of bounds. She could visit and inspect any cell, kitchen, dining area, recreation area or anywhere else.

5A was not interested in an inspection.

All she was interested in was to see where prisoner 5940 had spent most of his time and talk to the people who knew him best. Fellow inmates, prison guards and anybody else with whom he had close contact.

Her tour began with a visit to the isolation area where CAT2 prisoners were held.

She met his gay cellmate. They talked at some length about the time 5940 spent inside and how he had inspired others with his positive attitude. She made notes.

She learned that prisoner 5940 never gave up hope.

He would tell people that life inside could be made more bearable and even rewarding, but only if they believed it possible. 'You have to *believe* it before you *see* it 'was his philosophy. A philosophy that went over most people's heads.

He often used analogies to make a point. Smoking and dieting were two he used frequently.

He said anybody could achieve any goal if they wanted it enough, adding, but you must *believe* it before you *see* it.

The gay cellmate said that he'd met hundreds of prisoners over the years and without exception, they had all been wrongfully imprisoned.

Only his friend, prisoner 5940 had convinced him that he was a true victim of justice.

At one time, early into the 12-year sentence, a rumour began to spread that the wife had perhaps disappeared on purpose.

When he confronted 5940 with the rumour and suggested she might have had a hidden agenda, he was given short shrift.

'What? My wife stitch me up? Why would she do that?

No, no chance. We've been together over 10 years and, trust me, if that were remotely true, I would have known'.

The subject was never raised again.

In an attempt to break up the conversation between the VIP and the inmate, the Superintendent announced: 'We're having a service for him today. You'd be welcome to join us'.

That brought proceedings to an abrupt halt.

'Service? What sort of service?' 5A enquired.

'A memorial service. Some of the prisoners felt they'd like to mark his passing with a service of remembrance'.

'A memorial service? I don't understand. Who for?

'Oh, I'm sorry. Prisoner 5940 died. I thought you knew. I thought that's why you came here, to piece together his final years'.

The VIP guest looked shocked and listened as the Superintendent carried on.

'I received a letter from his lawyer, Richard Dadson. He wrote to say that Michael Hanson died in a car accident in Sheboygan in upstate Wisconsin'.

5A said nothing. She was stunned into silence and then, as she pulled herself together, said:

'Please go on. When did it happen?'

'About two weeks ago. The lawyer says he thinks he may have moved over to the wrong side of the road. His car was in the left lane, facing oncoming traffic but that no other vehicle was involved.

I have the letter in my office. I'm sorry. I just assumed you knew'.

'No. I had no idea. I'd like to see the letter'.

'It's not a letter as such. It's an email.

Back in his office he handed her a copy. She saw that it was dated Thursday 18th June 2015.

She would have been en route to India. Probably at Heathrow airport in transit.

'You can keep it if you like'.

She didn't answer. She read the words slowly and carefully.

Dear Superintendent,

It is with sincere regret and a heavy heart that I write to inform you that one of my clients, Mr Michael Hanson whom you know as prisoner 5940, was recently involved in an auto accident and died at the scene. No other car was involved.

The police believe he may have been driving on the wrong side of the road.

He leaves no relatives.

Towards the end of the email Dadson went on to say:

I am attending to his affairs.

In his last Will and Testament, which I drew up for him shortly after we met, is a clause which I need to bring to your attention.

It concerns a list of final wishes, one of which addresses concerns he had for prisoners being held in Goa prison.

My client has set aside the sum $250,000 dollars, to be donated to the charity Amnesty International.

The donation is subject to certain conditions.

The money can only be used to support families of qualifying prisoners living at Goa prison.

The bequest will be listed in the charities accounts as 'restricted funds'.

If you would like to know how the fund may be accessed, and the rules of qualification, please let me know and I will put you in touch with the appropriate department at Amnesty International.

Yours,

Richard Dadson

5A folded the copy and put it inside her purse.

'You have been most kind and helpful but I feel I must get back to Los Angeles. I need to find out about the funeral'.

'Oh dear. That won't be possible. The funeral has already been held' added the Superintendent.

'As there were no suspicious circumstances the coroner returned a verdict of "accidental death".

His body was cremated with the ashes scattered in the garden of remembrance. He had no relatives.

'That's all I know. If you need any more information I suggest you contact Mr Dadson.

5A cut short her visit and headed for the airport in a government courtesy car, similar to the one that carried 5940 when he left prison for the same journey to the airport.

By the time she arrived back in Los Angeles she'd already decided not to wait to be fired.

Armed with a letter of resignation she went straight to see her boss.

He was too busy. His secretary, looking rather sheepish, explained that he would be tied up in meetings all day, but that she had two envelopes for her.

One envelope carried the familiar CNN logo. It had her name typed on the front. Ms Angela Lomax - and was stamped 'strictly private and confidential'. He'd beaten her to it.

The second envelope was handwritten. To 5A from 5B. Personal.

As the secretary handed it over she explained: 'This was handed in at Reception a few days ago'.

The gentleman didn't ask for you by name but asked for it to be handed to the English reporter.

You're the only one we have…or rather, had.

CHAPTER 19   Back from the dead

After the memorial service had ended, Monica went home to be on her own.

The home was much too big for a single occupant, but she had no plans to move.

This had been home for 20 plus years and was full of happy memories. It was warm in the winter and cool in the summer and mortgage free.

She had caring neighbours who had been a great comfort when her husband Geoff passed away.

His body had eventually succumbed to the cancer that he'd lived with for five years.

She began looking through an old photograph album.

Each photograph captured a frozen moment in time.

Good times that she and husband Geoff had shared with their neighbours.

They included summers and Christmas and Thanksgiving parties.

She looked longingly at one with a Christmas tree in the background.

Geoff stood to the left of the tree, wearing a Santa hat.

She wore an apron with a picture of a reindeer, and Michael and Emily were in the background sipping wine.

She gently ran her fingers over the images. A tear ran down her cheek at the thought of four people being reduced to just one. Geoff had died. Emily had disappeared and Michael hadn't been heard of for years. He could also be dead for all she knew.

She smiled to herself as she recalled how Michael proclaimed that he'd never met an American who could make a decent cup of tea. They never knew whether to put the milk in first or last, or why it mattered.

There was a photograph of the guys cooking on a barbecue as they watched the Super Bowl on a TV, rigged up on the porch.

Michael was extremely well-read and would often quote from a favourite book.

He would have them in fits of laughter when he exaggerated his British accent.

'Aunt Patience, you make me as cross as two sticks'.

He would always end a quote with the name of the author or book or film from which it came.

'That my dears was from Daphne du Maurier's book, Jamaica Inn'.

Quick as a flash Geoff's response was; *'Frankly my dear, I don't give a damn. Clark Gable – Gone with the Wind'.*

They enjoyed a magical friendship.

The silence was suddenly interrupted by the phone ringing.

She slowly turned the album over to save the page she was on, and walked across the room, rather hoping the ringing would stop before she reached the phone.

She raised the phone to her ear. Half a second later a male voice said: 'Monica?'

Stunned, she knew in an instant that it was Michael.

'Michael? Is that you? Is that *really* you?

Where are you?

Were you at the service?

Are you calling from India?

How are you?

Speak to me...

Flustered she cried: 'Oh I'm sorry. I don't know what to say. I have to sit down'.

Five seconds of silence followed, and then, just as Monica was about to speak, Michael whispered:

'I'm sorry Monica. I'm outside'.

Monica was in a daze. She ran to the window. Michael stood by the front door holding a mobile phone to his ear, waiting for her response.

She was already running to the front door and instinctively glanced at the mirror, hand brushed her hair and ran her tongue over her lips.

She got to the door and frantically unlocked it. As she did she pulled it open to see Michael standing alone.

Neither knew what to do or say next.

They both went forward at the same time and hugged. Tears welled up in their eyes.

Michael began: 'I wasn't sure if I should come here without letting you know first'.

'Don't just stand there. Come in'.

For the next two hours they hardly paused for breath, and when they did, they held each other's hands so as not to break the spell.

So much had happened over such a long period, neither knew quite what to say. There was just so much to tell.

No, he hadn't been to the memorial service. He didn't even know about it.

Yes, he had been convicted of murder and no, he didn't do it.

Staccato sentences in rapid fire.

As the pace slowed down, they sat looking into each other's eyes. Neither knowing what to say or do next.

Monica broke the silence: 'Would you like a cup of tea?' The both laughed.

'Yes. I'd like that. Let me help you'.

'I haven't known what it's like to speak to a real friend for such a long time', said Michael with a sigh.

'Tell me about it' said Monica.

While they rekindled their friendship, an unsuspecting Emily Hanson went back to her mobile home, still wondering why her husband hadn't bothered to show up at her memorial service.

CHAPTER 20   A toast to Ben.

Red Bay Beach - Cayman Islands.

A man and a woman can be seen standing together, on a wooden jetty overlooking a white sandy beach as they stared at the horizon.

A light aircraft appeared and began its descent.

One of them, the man, reached for a pair of binoculars and passed them to his companion. She studied the aircraft and nodded.

As it approached, the outline of water landing skis could be seen hanging below the fuselage. A seaplane is an unusual sight, even in the Cayman Islands.

This aircraft was painted bright yellow and blue. A De Havilland twin engine Otter; popular with tourists in Vancouver and Miami.

The couple continued to watch as the experienced pilot made a perfect touchdown on the crystal clear waters of the Caribbean.

The aircraft taxied towards the jetty. On the side of the fuselage were the words: Lomax Airways.

The tail fin displayed an ID number painted yellow on a blue background...5A.

The pilot cut the engine and stepped out onto one of the landing skis.

She removed a familiar looking pair of oversize sunglasses and looked across to the couple waiting to greet her.

The female pilot got into a waiting row boat and was ferried to the shore.

Michael began the introductions:

'Monica. Meet 5A'.

'5A meet Monica'.

'Michael, can we drop the numbers?'

Monica, I do have a name. I'm Angela Lomax.

'Angela, I've heard a lot about you'.

'You tell me what he said, and I'll let you know if I agree'.

After warm embraces all round they joined hands and walked to the beachside restaurant where a seafood platter, pre-ordered by Michael, was waiting for them.

Towards the end of lunch, Michael gestured to his two companions to raise their glasses.

'I'd like to propose a toast'.

'To Ben. Whoever you are and wherever you are. I owe you my life'.

Startled, his two companions said in unison:

'Ben? Who is Ben?'.

'Ben the benefactor. He needed a name, so I chose Ben'.

'You think Ben's a man? asked Monica.

'I have no idea'. I quite like the idea of not knowing and leaving it as a mystery – unsolved.

All I hope is that Ben is being well rewarded for everything he did'.

With beaming smiles, they raised their glasses;

'To Ben'.

At that very moment, somewhere in Lovelock, Nevada sat a lonely woman, looking 10 years older than her natural years.

She had a decision to make.

In front of her was a crumpled five-dollar bill and some loose change.

She counted the coins and pondered the choice.

Should she buy the large milk and a single line on a Lotto ticket, or a small milk and two lines?

Characters:

Emily

In the beginning, Emily planned her disappearance with military precision.

She wanted to punish her husband for having an affair with her best friend.

She knew that choosing Goa as a holiday destination would be an inspired choice.

That alone would point the finger of suspicion at her husband.

She would leave nothing to chance, or so she thought.

The embittered Emily hadn't considered that one of the consequences of the failed plot was that her husband could go to jail.

Only after the jail sentence came to light, did she realise that her plan had backfired with terrible consequences.

Knowing that if she came out of hiding she would be sent back to India to face trial and a long jail sentence. She decided to remain 'missing presumed dead' and use her anonymity to become an anonymous benefactor.

Her elaborate and bogus memorial service was designed to ensure that if anybody tried try to track her down, the search would end there.

Most of her ill-gotten gains went to pay Dadson, her lawyer, which left her with just enough money to buy a static home on a trailer park in aptly named Lovelock, a small town in Nevada with a population of 1903.

Ironically, her actions led to her husband and her best friend being thrown together.

She never found out what happened to him after him after his release.

5A

It was pure chance that led to 5A being seated next to Michael Hanson on the flight from London to Los Angeles.

During the flight she gave no hint or clue that she was a journalist. As she listened to his story of life behind bars for a crime he hadn't committed, she saw an opportunity for a front page headline story.

It all went wrong when her fellow passenger accidentally spotted her on the news channel.

When Hanson didn't show up to meet her boss she was despatched to meet his lawyer. When that didn't work she went half way round the world to India only to hear that Hanson was already dead and buried.

Hanson had some sympathy for 5A and realised that he had much to do with her downfall.

While she was on her abortive trip to India he delivered a handwritten envelope to the CNN offices. Inside was a cheque and a letter of apology.

Giving her $1miilion out of the six million compensation wouldn't be noticed.

5A used the money to start her own air charter business based in Miami, Lomax Airways.

Richard Dadson

Sceptical at first, Dadson accepted the challenge to get Emily's husband's case reviewed, with spectacular success.

The upfront payment of $50,000 from the anonymous benefactor helped him make up his mind.

During the months that he corresponded with prisoner 5940 he became convinced that the man might actually be innocent.

Dadson was complicit in allowing the story of Michael Hanson's accident to filter through to the local press. Hanson asked his advice on creating a new identity.

Dadson honoured the wishes of the anonymous benefactor and never attempted to establish his or her identity, although he did have his suspicions.

Monica

Monica was happily married to Geoff and never did have an affair with Michael.

Emily's suspicions were unfounded. The first seeds of doubt were sewn when Monica joined the same golf club that Michael was already a member of.

When Michael invited Monica to partner him in a mixed competition, Emily was fuming but said nothing.

Over the next 12 months her suspicions grew and she decided that they weren't just playing a round together, they were playing around, together.

Confrontation would lead to denial. The love she once held for her husband had long since died.

Her religious upbringing was the foundation of the belief that adultery was a mortal sin which had to be punished.

Emily Hanson's hatred manifested itself into a devious plot to exact revenge, part of which was that neither of them would know why they were being persecuted.

For years the two families had been close neighbours and visited each other's houses on a regular basis.

While Michael was incarcerated in prison, Geoff died of cancer.

She'd seen her own husband buried and attended Emily's memorial service.

Monica was left all alone in the world...until the phone call.

5B, 5940, Michael Hanson.

Three years in prison and with no contact from his missing wife, prisoner 5940 came to accept that she was indeed 'missing presumed dead'.

With the help of his lawyer Richard Dadson, he had become a wealthy man.

He rewarded Angela Lomax aka 5A with $1 million dollars enabling her to buy a light aircraft and start her own private air charter business.

He would honour the request of his benefactor never to attempt to track him or her down.

The unintended consequence of the actions of his wife led to Michael Hanson to be a free man, in every sense of the word.

ABOUT THE AUTHOR

After a successful business career as CEO of organisations in manufacturing, retailing and management consultancy, John became a senior lecturer at the IoD (Institute of Directors) in London, England.

After retiring, he turned his hand to writing self-help books.

Titles include:

- **Top Tips: Interviewing**
- **Top Tips: Writing a CV/Resume**
- **The Interview Bible**
- **Test Your Financial Awareness**
- **Where to Find Things When I'm Gone**.

Guilty Until Proved Innocent is his debut short story, available as a paperback on Amazon or e-book worldwide.

He lives with his wife Anyta in Cambridge, England.

They have three children and eight grandchildren.

Hobbies include travelling, eating out, playing golf and fly-fishing.

He is a passionate supporter and fund-raiser of the Arthur Rank Hospice Charity.

Printed in Great Britain
by Amazon

19642137R00080